Dinah Maria Mulock Craik

A Noble Life

Vol. 1

Dinah Maria Mulock Craik

A Noble Life
Vol. 1

ISBN/EAN: 9783337779986

Printed in Europe, USA, Canada, Australia, Japan

Cover: Foto ©Andreas Hilbeck / pixelio.de

More available books at **www.hansebooks.com**

A NOBLE LIFE.

BY

THE AUTHOR OF

"JOHN HALIFAX, GENTLEMAN,"

"CHRISTIAN'S MISTAKE,"

&c. &c.

FIAT VOLUNTAS TUA.

IN TWO VOLUMES.

VOL. I.

LONDON:

HURST AND BLACKETT, PUBLISHERS,

13, GREAT MARLBOROUGH STREET.

1866.

Dedicated,

WITH THE AFFECTION OF EIGHTEEN YEARS,

TO

UNCLE GEORGE.

Chapter the First.

ANY years ago, how many need not be recorded, there lived in his ancestral castle, in the far north of Scotland, the last Earl of Cairnforth.

You will not find his name in "Lodge's Peerage," for, as I say, he was the last Earl, and with him the title became extinct. It had been borne for centuries by many noble and gallant men, who had lived worthily or died bravely. But I think amongst what we call "heroic" lives — lives, the story of which touches us with something higher than pity and deeper than love,

— there never was any of his race who left behind a history more truly heroic than he.

Now that it is all over and done — now that the soul so mysteriously given has gone back unto Him who gave it, and a little green turf in the kirk-yard behind Cairnforth Manse covers the poor body in which it dwelt for more than forty years, I feel it might do good to many, and would do harm to none, if I related the story — a very simple one, and more like a biography than a tale — of Charles Edward Stuart Montgomerie, last Earl of Cairnforth.

He did not succeed to the title; he was born Earl of Cairnforth; his father having been drowned in the loch a month before — the wretched Countess herself beholding the sight from her Castle windows. She lived but to know she had a son and heir — to whom she desired might be given his father's name: then she died—more glad than sorry to depart, for she had loved her husband all her life, and had only been married to him a year. Perhaps, had she once seen her son, she might have wished less to die than to live, if only for his sake:—however, it was not God's will that this should be. So, at two days old, the "poor little Earl"—as from his very birth people began compassionately to call him—was left alone in the world, without a single near relative or connection—his parents having both been only children;—but with his title, his estate, and twenty thousand a-year.

Cairnforth Castle is one of the loveliest residences in all Scotland. It is built on the extremity of a long tongue of land which stretches out between two salt-water lochs — Loch Beg, the " little," and Loch Mhor, the " big " lake. The latter is grand and gloomy, shut in by bleak mountains, which sit all round it, their feet in the water, and their heads in mist and cloud. But Loch Beg is quite different. It has green, cultivated, sloping shores, fringed with trees to the water's edge ; and the least ray of sunshine seems always to set it dimpling with wavy smiles. Now and then a sudden squall comes down from the chain of mountains far away beyond the head of the loch, and then its waters begin to darken —just like a sudden frown over a bright face; the waves curl and rise, and lash themselves into foam, and any little sailing boat, which has been happily and safely riding over them five minutes before, is often struck and capsized immediately. Thus it happened when the late Earl was drowned.

The minister—the Rev. Alexander Cardross—had been out sailing with him; had only just landed, and was watching the boat crossing back again, when the squall came down. Though this region is a populous district now, with white villas dotted like daisies all along the green shores, there was then not a house in the whole peninsula of Cairnforth except the Castle, the Manse, and a few cottages, called the " clachan." Before help was possible, the Earl and his boatman, Neil

Campbell, were both drowned. The only person saved was little Malcolm Campbell—Neil's brother—a boy about ten years old.

In most country parishes of Scotland or England there is an almost superstitious feeling that "the minister," or "the clergyman," must be the fittest person to break any terrible tidings. So it ought to be. Who but the messenger of God should know best how to communicate His awful will, as expressed in great visitations of calamity? In this case no one could have been more suited for his solemn office than Mr. Cardross. He went up to the Castle door, as he had done to that of many a cottage, bearing the same solemn message of sudden death, to which there could be but one answer—"Thy will be done."

But the particulars of that terrible interview, in which he had to tell the Countess what already her own eyes had witnessed — though they refused to believe the truth — the minister never repeated to any creature except his wife. And afterwards, during the four weeks that Lady Cairnforth survived her husband, he was the only person, beyond her necessary attendants, who saw her until she died.

The day after her death he was suddenly summoned to the Castle by Mr. Menteith, an Edinburgh writer to the signet, and confidential agent, or factor, as the office is called in Scotland, to the late Earl.

" They'll be sending for you to baptize the child. It's early — but the puir bit thing may be delicate, and they may want it done at once, before Mr. Menteith returns to Edinburgh."

" May be so, Helen ; so do not expect me back till you see me."

Thus saying, the minister quitted his sunshiny manse garden, where he was working peacefully among his raspberry-bushes, with his wife looking on,—and walked, in meditative mood, through the Cairnforth woods, now blue with hyacinths in their bosky shadows, and in every nook and corner starred with great clusters of yellow primroses, which in this part of the country grow profusely, even down to within a few feet of high-water mark, on the tidal shores of the lochs. Their large, round, smiling faces, so irresistibly suggestive of baby smiles at sight of them, and baby fingers clutching at them, touched the heart of the good minister, who had left two small creatures of his own — a " bit girlie " of five, and a two-year-old boy — playing on his grass-plot at home with some toys of the Countess's giving; she had always been exceedingly kind to the Manse children.

He thought of her, lying dead; and then of her poor little motherless and father-less baby, whom, if she had any conscious-ness in her death-hour, it must have been a sore pang to her to leave behind. And the tears gathered again and again in the good man's eyes — shutting out from his vision all the beauty of the spring.

He reached the grand Italian portico, built by some former Earl with a taste for that style, and yet harmonising well with the smooth lawn, bounded by a circle of magnificent trees, through which came glimpses of the glittering loch. The great doors used almost always to stand open, and the windows were rarely closed — the Countess liked sunshine and fresh air, but now all was shut up and silent, and not a soul was to be seen about the place.

Mr. Cardross sighed, and walked round to the other side of the Castle, where was my lady's flower-garden, or what was to be made into one. Then he entered by French windows, from a terrace overlooking it, my lord's library, also incomplete. For the Earl, who was by no means a bookish man, had only built that room since his marriage, to please his wife, whom perhaps he loved all the better that she was so exceedingly unlike himself. Now, both were away,— their short dream of married life ended, their plans and hopes crumbled into dust. As yet, no external changes had been made — the other solemn changes having come so suddenly. Gardeners still worked in the parterres, and masons and carpenters still, in a quiet and lazy manner, went on completing the beautiful room ; but there was no one to order them ; no one watched their work. Except for workmen the place seemed so deserted, that Mr. Cardross wandered through the house for some time before he found a single servant to direct him to the person of whom he was in search.

Mr. Menteith sat alone in a little room filled with guns and fishing-rods, and ornamented with stag's heads, stuffed birds, and hunting relics of all sorts, which had been called, not too appropriately, the Earl's "study." He was a little, dried-up man, about fifty years old, of sharp but not unkindly aspect. When the minister entered, he looked up from the mass of papers which he seemed to have been trying to reduce into some kind of order—apparently the late Earl's private papers, which had been untouched since his death, for there was a sad and serious shadow over what would otherwise have been rather a humorous face.

"Welcome, Mr. Cardross! I am indeed glad to see you. I took the liberty of sending for you, since you are the only person with whom I can consult — we can consult, I should say, for Dr. Hamilton wished it likewise — on this — this most painful occasion."

"I shall be very glad to be of the slightest service," returned Mr. Cardross. "I had the utmost respect for those that are away." He had a habit, this tender-hearted, pious man, who, with all his learning, kept a religious faith as simple as a child's, of always speaking of the dead as only "away."

The two gentlemen sat down together. They had often met before, for whenever there were guests at Cairnforth Castle, the Earl always invited the minister and his wife to dinner, but they had never fraternised much. Now, a common sympathy, nay, more, a common grief — for something beyond sympathy, keen personal regret, was evidently felt by both for the departed Earl and Countess — made them suddenly familiar.

"Is the child doing well?" was Mr. Cardross's first and most natural question; but it seemed to puzzle Mr. Menteith exceedingly.

"I suppose so — indeed, I can hardly say. This is a most difficult and painful matter."

"It was born alive, and is a son and heir, as I heard?"

"Yes."

"That is fortunate."

"For some things; since had it been

a girl, the title would have lapsed, and the long line of Earls of Cairnforth ended. At one time Dr. Hamilton feared the child would be stillborn, and then, of course, the earldom would have been extinct. The property must in that case have passed to the Earl's distant cousins, the Bruces, of whom you may have heard, Mr. Cardross?"

"I have; and there are few things, I fancy, which Lord Cairnforth would have regretted more than such heirship."

"You are right," said the keen W. S., evidently relieved. "It was my instinctive conviction that you were in the late Earl's confidence on this point, which made me decide to send and consult with you. We must take all precautions, you see. We are placed in a most painful and responsible position, — both Dr. Hamilton and myself."

It was now Mr. Cardross's turn to look perplexed. No doubt it was a most sad fatality which had happened, but still things did not seem to warrant the excessive anxiety testified by Mr. Menteith.

"I do not quite comprehend you. There might have been difficulties as to the succession, but are they not all solved by the birth of a healthy, living heir — whom we must cordially hope will long continue to live?"

"I hardly know if we ought to hope it," said the lawyer, very seriously. "But we must 'keep a calm sough' on that matter for the present — so far, at least, Dr. Hamilton and I have determined — in order to prevent the Bruces from getting wind of it. Now, then, will you come and see the Earl?"

"The Earl!" re-echoed Mr. Cardross with a start; then recollected himself, and sighed to think how one goes and another comes, and all the world moves on as before — passing, generation after generation, into the awful shadow which no eye except that of faith can penetrate. Life is a little, little day! — hardly longer, in the end, for the man in his prime than for the infant of an hour's span.

And the minister, who was of meditative mood, thought to himself much as a poet half a century later put into words — thoughts common to all men — but which only such a man and such a

poet could have crystallised into four such
perfect lines :

"Thou wilt not leave us in the dust:
　Thou madest man, he knows not why;
　He thinks he was not made to die,
And Thou hast made him—Thou art just."

Thus musing, Mr. Cardross followed up-
stairs towards the magnificent nursery, which
had been prepared months before, with a
loving eagerness of anticipation, and a merciful blindness to futurity, for the expected
heir of the Earls of Cairnforth. For, as
before said, the only hope of the lineal
continuance of the race was in this one
child. It lay in a cradle resplendent with
white satin hangings and lace curtains, and
beside it sat the nurse — a mere girl, but

a widow already — Neil Campbell's widow, whose first child had been born only two days after her husband was drowned. Mr. Cardross knew that she had been suddenly sent for out of the clachan, the Countess having, with her dying breath, desired that this young woman, whose circumstances were so like her own, should be taken as wet-nurse to the new-born baby.

So, in her widow's weeds, grave and sad, but very sweet-looking — she had been a servant at the Castle, and was a rather superior young woman — Janet Campbell took her place beside her charge, with an expression in her face as if she felt it was a charge left her by her lost mistress, which must be kept solemnly to the end of her days. — As it was.

The minister shook hands with her silently—she had gone through sore affliction—but the lawyer addressed her in his quick, sharp, business tone, under which he often disguised more emotion than he liked to show.

"You have not been dressing the child? Dr. Hamilton told you not to attempt it."

"Na, na, sir, I didna try," answered Janet, sadly and gently.

"That was well. I'm a father of a family myself," added Mr. Menteith, more gently: "I've six of them; but, thank the Lord, ne'er a one of them like this. Take it on your lap, nurse, and let the minister look at it! Ay, here comes Dr. Hamilton!"

Mr. Cardross knew Dr. Hamilton by repute — as who did not? since at that period it was the widest-known name in the whole medical profession in Scotland. And the first sight of him confirmed the reputation, and made even a stranger recognise that his fame was both natural and justifiable. But the minister had scarcely time to cast a glance on the acute, benevolent, wonderfully powerful and thoughtful head, when his attention was attracted by the poor infant, whom Janet was carefully unswathing from innumerable folds of cotton wool.

Mrs. Campbell was a widow of only a month, and her mistress, to whom she had been much attached, lay dead in the next room, yet she had still a few tears left, and they were dropping like rain over her mistress's child.

No wonder. It lay on her lap, the smallest, saddest specimen of infantile deformity. It had a large head — larger than most infants have—but its body was thin, elfish, and distorted, every joint and limb being twisted in some way or other. You could not say that any portion of the child was natural or perfect, except the head and face. Whether it had the power of motion or not seemed doubtful; at any rate it made no attempt to move, except feebly turning its head from side to side. It lay, with its large eyes wide open, and at last opened its poor little mouth also, and uttered a loud pathetic wail.

"It greets, doctor, ye hear," said the

nurse, eagerly; "'Deed, an' it greets fine, whiles."

"A good sign," observed Dr. Hamilton. "Perhaps it may live after all; though one scarcely knows whether to desire it."

"I'll gar it live, doctor," cried Janet, as she rocked and patted it, and at last managed to lay it to her motherly breast; "I'll gar it live, ye'll see! That is, God willing."

"It could not live, it could never have lived at all, if He were *not* willing," said the minister reverently. And then, after a long pause — during which he and the two other gentlemen stood watching, with sad pitying looks, the unfortunate child — he added, so quietly and naturally that though they might have thought it odd, they could hardly have thought it out of place or hypocritical, " Let us pray."

It was a habit, long familiar to this good Presbyterian minister, who went in and out among his parishioners as their pastor and teacher, consoler and guide. Many a time, in many a cottage, had he knelt down, just as he did here, in the midst of deep affliction, and said a few simple words, as from children to a father — the Father of all men. And the beginning and end of his prayer was, now as always, the expression and experience of his own entire faith — " Thy will be done."

" But what ought *we* to do ? " said

the Edinburgh writer, when having quitted, not unmoved, the melancholy nursery, he led the way to the scarcely less dreary dining - room, where the two handsome, bright - looking portraits of the late Earl and Countess still smiled down from the wall — giving Mr. Cardross a start, and making him recall, as if the intervening six weeks had been all a dream, the last day he and Mr. Menteith dined together at that hospitable table. They stole a look at one another, but, with true Scotch reticence, neither exchanged a word. Yet, perhaps, each respected the other the more, both for the feeling and for its instant repression.

"Whatever we decide to do, ought to be decided now," said Dr. Hamilton, "for I must be in Edinburgh to-morrow. And, besides, it is a case in which no medical skill is of much avail, if any: nature must struggle through — or yield: which I cannot help thinking would be the best ending. In Sparta, now, this poor child would have been exposed on Mount — what was the place? to be saved by any opportune death from the still greater misfortune of living."

"But that would have been murder,— sheer murder," earnestly replied the minister. "And we are not Spartans, but Christians: to whom the body is not everything, and who believe that God can work out His wonderful will, if He chooses, through the meanest means — through the saddest tragedies, and direst misfortunes. In one sense,

Dr. Hamilton, there is no such thing as evil — that is, there is no actual evil in the world except sin."

"There is plenty of that, alas!" said Mr. Menteith. "But as to the child, I wished you to see it — both of you together — if only to bear evidence as to its present condition. For the late Earl, by his will, executed, by a most providential chance, the last time I was here, appointed me sole guardian and trustee to a possible widow or child. On me, therefore, depends the charge of this poor infant — the sole bar between those penniless, grasping, altogether discreditable Bruces, and the large property of Cairnforth. You see my position, gentlemen?"

It was not an easy one, and no wonder the honest man looked much troubled.

"I need not say that I never sought it — never thought it possible it would really fall to my lot: but it has fallen, and I must discharge it to the best of my ability. You see what the Earl is — born alive, anyhow — though we can hardly wish him to survive.

The three gentlemen were silent. At length Mr. Cardross said,—

"There is one worse doubt which has occurred to me. Do you think, Dr. Hamilton, that the mind is as imperfect as the body? In short, is it not likely that the poor child may turn out to be an idiot?"

"I do not know; and it will be almost impossible to judge for months yet."

"But idiot or not," cried Mr. Menteith —a regular old Tory, who clung with true conservative veneration to the noble race which he, his father, and grandfather, had served faithfully for a century and more— "Idiot or not, the boy is undoubtedly Earl of Cairnforth."

"Poor child!"

The gentlemen then sat down, and thoroughly discussed the whole matter : finally deciding that, until things appeared somewhat plainer, it was advisable to keep the Earl's condition as much as possible from the world in general, and more especially from his own kindred. The Bruces —who lived abroad, would, it was naturally to be concluded — or Mr. Menteith, who had a lawyer's slender faith in human nature, believed so — would pounce down, like eagles upon a wounded lamb, the instant they heard what a slender thread of life hung between them and these great possessions.

Under such circumstances, for the infant to be left unprotected in the solitudes of Loch Beg was very unadvisable; and besides it was the guardian's duty to see that every aid which medical skill and surgical science could procure, was supplied to a child so afflicted, and upon whose life so much depended. He therefore proposed, and Dr. Hamilton agreed, that immediately after the funeral, the little Earl should be taken to Edinburgh, and there placed in the house of the latter, to remain there a year or two, or so long as might be necessary.

Janet Campbell was called in, and expressed herself willing to take her share — no small one — in the responsibility of this plan, if the minister would see to her "ain bairn;" if the minister really thought the scheme a wise one.

"The minister's opinion seems to carry great weight here," said Dr. Hamilton, smiling.

And it was so : not merely because of his being a minister, but because, with all his gentle, unassuming ways, he had an excellent judgment — the clear, sound, unbiassed judgment which no man can ever attain to except a man who thinks little of himself: to whom his own honour and glory come ever second, and his Master's glory and service first. Therefore, both as a man and a minister, Mr. Cardross was equally and wholly reliable : charitable, because he felt his own infirmities ; placing himself at no higher level than his neighbour, he was always calmly and scrupulously just. Though a learned, he was not exactly a clever man : probably his sermons, preached every Sunday for the last ten years in Cairnforth Kirk, were neither better nor worse than the generality of country sermons ;—but that matters little. He was a wise man and a good man, and all his parishioners — scattered over a parish of fourteen Scotch miles — deeply and dearly loved him.

"I think," said Mr. Cardross, "that this plan has many advantages, and is, under the circumstances, the best that could have been devised. True, I should like to have had the poor babe under my own eye and my wife's, that we might try to requite in some degree the many kindnesses we have received from his poor father and mother:—but he will be better off in Edinburgh. Give him every possible chance of life and health, and a sound mind, and then we must leave the rest to Him, who would not have sent this poor little one into the world at all if He had not had some purpose in so doing, though what that purpose is we cannot see. I suppose we shall see it, and many other dark things—some time."

The minister lifted his grave, gentle eyes, and sat looking out upon the familiar view—the sunshiny loch, the green shore, and the far-away circle of mountains—while the other two gentlemen discussed a few other business matters. Then he invited them both to return with him and dine at the Manse, where he and his wife were accustomed to offer to all comers, high and low, rich and poor, "hospitality without grudging."

So the three walked through Cairnforth woods, now glowing with full spring beauty, and wandered about the minister's garden till dinner-time. It was a very simple meal—just the ordinary family dinner, as it was spread day after day, all the year round:—they could afford hospitality, but show, with the minister's limited income, was impossible; and he was too honest to attempt it. Many a time the Earl himself had dined, merrily and heartily, at that simple table—with the mistress, active, energetic, cheerful, and refined, sitting at the head of it — and the children, a girl and boy, already admitted to take their place there, quiet and well-behaved — brought up from the first to be, like their parents, gentlemen and gentlewomen. The Manse table was a perfect picture of family sunshine and family peace; and, as such, the two Edinburgh guests carried away the impression of it in their memories for many a day.

In another week a second stately funeral passed out of the Castle doors, and then they were closed to all comers. By Mr. Menteith's orders, great part of the rooms were shut up, and only two apartments kept for his own use when he came down to look after the estates. It was now fully known that he was the young Earl's sole guardian;

but so great was the feudal fidelity of the neighbourhood, and so entire the respect with which, during an administration of many years, the factor had imbued the Cairnforth tenantry, that not a word was said in objection either to him or to his doings. There was great regret that the poor little Earl — the representative of so long and honoured a race — was taken away from the admiration of the country-side before even a single soul in the parish — except Mr. and Mrs. Cardross — had set eyes upon him; but still the disappointed gossips submitted, considering that if the minister were satisfied all must be right.

After the departure of Mr. Menteith, Mrs. Campbell, and her charge, a few rumours got abroad that the little Earl was "no a' richt" — if an Earl could be " no richt " — which the simple folk about Loch Beg and Loch Mhor, accustomed for generations to view the Earls of Cairnforth much as the Thibetians view their Dalai Lama, thought hardly possible. But what was wrong with him nobody precisely knew. The minister did, it was conjectured ; but Mr. Cardross was scrupulously silent on the subject ; and, with all his gentleness, he was the sort of man to whom nobody ever could address intrusive or impertinent questions.

So after a while, when the Castle still remained shut up, curiosity died out ; or was only roused at intervals, especially at Mr. Menteith's periodical visits. And to all questions, whether respectfully anxious, or merely inquisitive, he never gave but one answer — that the Earl was " doing pretty well," and would be back at Cairnforth " some o' these days."

However, that period was so long deferred, that the neighbours at last ceased to expect it, or to speculate concerning it. They went about their own affairs; and soon the whole story about the sad death of the late Earl and Countess, and the birth of the present nobleman, began to be told simply as a story by the elder folk, and slipped out of the younger ones' memories :—as, if one only allows it time, every tale, however sad, wicked, or strange, will very soon do. Had it not been for the silent, shut-up Castle, standing summer and winter on the lochside, with its flower-gardens blossoming for none to gather, and its woods — the pride of the whole country — budding and withering, with scarcely a foot to cross, or an eye to notice their wonderful beauty,—people would ere long have forgotten the very existence of the last Earl of Cairnforth.

Chapter the Second.

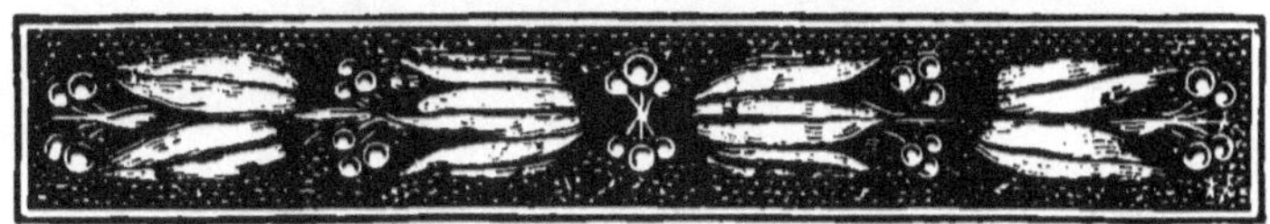

T was on a June day — ten years after that bright June day when the minister of Cairnforth had walked with such a sad heart up to Cairnforth Castle, and seen for the first time its unconscious heir — the poor little orphan baby who in such apparent mockery was called "the Earl." The woods, the hills, the loch, looked exactly the same — nature never changes. As Mr. Cardross walked up to the Castle once more, — the first time for many months, — in accordance with a request of Mr. Menteith's, who had written to say the Earl was coming home — he could hardly believe it was ten years since that sad week when the baby-heir was born, and the Countess's funeral had passed out from that now long-closed door.

Mr. Cardross's step was heavier and his face sadder now than then. He who had so often sympathised with others' sorrows, had had to suffer patiently his own. From the Manse gate, as from that of the Castle, the mother and mistress had been carried — never to return. A new Helen — only fifteen years old — was trying vainly to replace to father and brothers her who was — as Mr. Cardross still touchingly put it — "away." But though his grief was more than a year old, the minister mourned still. His was one of those quiet natures which make no show, and trouble no one, — yet in which sorrow goes deep down, and grows into the heart, as it were, becoming a part of existence, until existence itself shall cease.

It did not, however, hinder him from doing all his ordinary duties — perhaps with even closer persistence, as he felt himself sinking into that indifference to outside things, which is the inevitable result of a heavy loss upon any gentle nature. The fierce rebel against it ; the impetuous and impatient throw it off,— but the feeble and tender souls make no sign, only quietly pass into that state which the outer world calls submission and resignation, yet which is in truth mere passiveness — the stolid calm of a creature that has suffered till it can suffer no more.

The first thing which roused Mr. Cardross out of this condition, or at least the uneasy recognition that it was fast approaching, and must be struggled against, conscientiously, to the utmost of his power, —was Mr. Menteith's letter, and the request therein concerning Lord Cairnforth.

Without entering much into particulars — it was not the way of the cautious lawyer — he had stated, that after ten years' residence in Dr. Hamilton's house, and numerous consultations with every surgeon of repute in Scotland, England,—nay, Europe,— it had been decided, and especially at the earnest entreaty of the poor little Earl himself, to leave him to nature ; to take him back to his native air, and educate him, so far as was possible, in Cairnforth Castle.

A suitable establishment had accordingly been provided:—more servants, and a lady housekeeper or *gouvernante*, who took all external charge of the child, while the personal care of him was left, as before, to his nurse, Mrs. Campbell—now wholly devoted to him—for at seven years old her own boy had died. He had another attendant, to whom, with a curious persistency, he had strongly attached himself ever since his babyhood—young Malcolm Campbell, Neil Campbell's brother, who was saved by clinging to the keel of the boat, when the late Lord Cairnforth was drowned. Beyond these, whose fond fidelity knew no bounds, there was hardly need of any other person to take charge of the little Earl. Except a tutor—and that office Mr. Menteith entreated Mr. Cardross to accept.

It was a doubtful point with the minister. He shrank from assuming any new duty, his daily duties being now made only too heavy by the loss of the wife who had shared and lightened them all. But he named the matter to Helen, whom he had lately got into the habit of consulting,—she was such a wise little woman for her age; —and Helen said anxiously, " Papa, try." Besides, there were six boys to be brought up, and put out into the world somehow — and the Manse income was small, and the salary offered by Mr. Menteith very considerable. So when, the second time, Helen's great soft eyes implored silently, " Papa, please try," the minister kissed her, went into his study and wrote to Edinburgh his acceptance of the office of tutor to Lord Cairnforth.

What sort of office it would turn out—what kind of instruction he was expected to give, or how much the young Earl was capable of receiving, he had not the least idea; but he resolved that in any case he would do his duty, and neither man nor minister could be expected to do more.

In pursuance of this resolution he roused himself that sunny June morning, when he would far rather have sat over his study-fire and let the world go on without him —as he felt it would, easily enough ;— and walked down to the Castle, where, for the first time these ten years, windows were opened and doors unbarred, and the sweet

light and warm air of day let in upon those long-shut rooms, which seemed, in their dumb, inanimate way, glad to be happy again—glad to be made of use once more. Even the portraits of the late Earl and Countess—he in his Highland dress, and she in her white satin and pearls—both so young and bright; as they looked on the day they were married—seemed to gaze back at each other from either side the long dining-room, as if to say, rejoicingly, . "Our son is coming home."

"Have you seen the Earl?" said Mr. Cardross to one of the new servants who attended him round the rooms—listening respectfully to all the remarks and suggestions, as to furniture and the like, which Mr. Menteith had requested him to make. The minister was always specially popular with servants and inferiors of every sort; for he possessed, in a remarkable degree, that best key to their hearts — the gentle dignity which never needs to assert a superiority that is at once felt and acknowledged.

"The Earl, sir? Na, na," — with a mysterious shake of the head — "Naebody sees the Earl. Some say — but I hae nae cause to think it mysel' — that he's no a' there."

The minister was sufficiently familiar with that queer but very expressive Scotch phrase "not all there" — to pursue no further inquiries. But he sighed — and wished he had delayed a little before undertaking the tutorship. However, the matter was settled now. and Mr. Cardross was not the man ever to draw back from an agreement, or shrink from a promise.

"Whatever the poor child is—even if an idiot," thought he, "I will do my best for him—for his father's and mother's sake."

And he paused several minutes before those bright and smiling portraits, pondering on the mysterious dealings of the great Ruler of the universe—how some are taken and some are left: those removed who seem most happy and most needed; those left behind whom it would have appeared, in our dim and short-sighted judgment, a mercy—both to themselves and others—quietly to have taken away.

But one thing the minister did, in consequence of these somewhat sad and painful musings. On his return to the clachan, — where, of course, the news of the Earl's coming home had long spread, and thrown the whole country-side into a state of the greatest excitement, — he gave orders, or at least advice,—which was equivalent to orders, since everybody obeyed him — that there should be no special rejoicings on the Earl's coming home : no bonfire on the hill-side, or triumphal arches across the road, and at the ferry where the young Earl would probably land. Where, ten years before, the late Earl of Cairnforth had been, not landed, but carried, stone-cold, with his hair drip-ping, and his dead hands still clutching the weeds of the loch ;—the minister vividly re-called the sight and shuddered at it still.

" No, no," said he, in talking the matter over with some of his people, whom he went among like a father among his children, true pastor of a most loving flock —" No—we 'll wait and see what the Earl would like before we make any show. That we are glad to see him he knows well enough — or will very soon find out. And if he should arrive on such a night as this," — looking round on the magnificent June sunset, colouring the mountains at the head of the loch — "he will hardly need a brighter welcome to a bonnier home."

But the Earl did not arrive on a gorgeous evening like this—such as come sometimes to the shores of Loch Beg, and make it glow into a perfect paradise: he arrived in " saft " weather; in fact, on a pouring wet Saturday night; and all that the clachan saw of him was the outside of his carriage, driving, with closed blinds, down the hill-side. He had taken a long round, and had not crossed the ferry; and he was carried as fast as possible through the dripping wood, reaching, just as darkness fell, the Castle door.

Mr. Cardross, perhaps, should have been there to welcome the child — his conscience rather smote him that he was not; but it was the minister's unbroken habit of years to spend Saturday evening alone in his study. And it might be that, with a certain timidity inherent in his character, he shrank from this first meeting, and wished to put off as long as possible what must inevitably be awkward—and might be very painful. So, in darkness and rain, unwelcomed save by his own servants, most of whom even had never yet seen him, the poor little Earl came to his ancestral door.

But on Sunday morning all things were changed — with one of those sudden changes which make this part of the country so wonderfully beautiful, and so fascinating through its endless variety.

A perfect June day, with the loch glittering in the sun, and the hills beyond it softly outlined with the indistinctness that mountains usually wear in summer, but with the soft summer colouring, too, greenish-blue, lilac, and silver-grey, varying continually. In the woods behind, where the leaves were already gloriously green, the wood-pigeons were cooing, and the black-birds and mavises singing—just as if it had not been Sunday morning. Or rather as if

they knew it was Sunday, and were strain-
ing their tiny throats to bless the Giver of
sweet, peaceful, cheerful Sabbath-days — and
of all other good things, meant for man's
usage and delight.

At the portico of Cairnforth Castle —
for the first time since the hearse had
stood there — stood a carriage. One of
those large, roomy, splendid family-carriages
which were in use many years ago;
looking at it no passer-by could have the
slightest doubt that it was my Lord's
coach, and that my Lord sat therein in
solemn state, exacting and receiving an
amount of respect little short of veneration,
such as, for generations, the whole country-
side had always paid to the Earls of Cairnforth. This coach, though it was the

identical family coach, had been newly fur-
bished; its crimson satin glowed, and its
silver harness and ornaments flashed in the
sun: the coachman sat in his place, and two
footmen stood up in their places behind.
It was altogether a very splendid affair,
as became the equipage of a young nobleman who was known to possess twenty
thousand a-year; and who, from his Castle
tower — it had a tower, though nobody
ever climbed there — might, if he chose,
look around upon miles and miles of moorland, loch, hill-side, and cultivated land,
and say to himself — or be said to by his
nurse, as in the old song —

"These hills and these vales, from this tower that
    ye see,
They all shall belong, my young chieftain. to thee."

The horses pawed the ground for several minutes of delay, and then there appeared Mr. Menteith, followed by Mrs. Campbell — who was quite a grand lady now, in silks and satins — but with the same sweet, sad, gentle face. The lawyer and she stood aside, and made way for a big, stalwart young Highlander of about one-and-twenty or thereabouts, who carried in his arms, very gently and carefully, wrapped in a plaid, even although it was such a mild spring day, what looked like a baby, or a very young child.

" Stop a minute, Malcolm."

At the sound of that voice, which was not an infant's — though it was thin, and sharp, and unnatural rather for a boy — the big Highlander paused immediately.

" Hold me up higher — I want to look at the loch."

" Yes, my Lord."

This then — this poor, little, deformed figure, with every limb shrunken and useless, and every joint distorted, the head just able to sustain itself and turn feebly from one side to the other, and the thin white hands piteously twisted and help-less-looking—this, then, was the Earl of Cairnforth.

" It's a bonnie loch, Malcolm."

" It looks awfu' bonnie the day, my Lord."

" And," almost in a whisper, " was it just there my father was drowned ? "

" Yes, my Lord."

No one spoke, while the large, intelligent eyes, which seemed the principal feature of the thin face that rested against Malcolm's shoulder, looked out intently upon the loch.

Mrs. Campbell pulled her veil down, and wept a little. People said Neil Campbell had not been the best of husbands to her; but he was her husband; and she had never been back in Cairnforth till now; for her son had lived, died, and been buried away in Edinburgh.

At last Mr. Menteith suggested that the kirk-bell was beginning to ring.

" Very well — put me into the carriage."

Malcolm placed him, helpless as an infant, in a corner of the silken-padded coach, fitted with cushions especially suited for his comfort. There he sat — in his black velvet coat and point-lace collar, with silk stockings and dainty shoes upon the poor little feet that never had walked, and never would walk, in this world. The one bit of him that could be looked at without pain was his face, inherited from his beautiful mother. It was wan, pale, and much older than his years, but it was a sweet face — a lovely face : — so patient, thoughtful, — nay, strange to say, content. You could not look at it without a certain sense of peace, as if God, in taking away so much, had given something — which not many people have — something which was the divine answer to the minister's prayer over the two-days-old child, — " Thy will be done."

" Are you comfortable, my Lord ? "

" Quite, thank you, Mr. Menteith. Stop, where are you going, Malcolm ? "

" Just to the kirk, and I 'll be there as soon as your lordship."

" Very well," said the little Earl, and watched with wistful eyes the tall Highlander striding across brushwood and heather, leaping dykes and clearing fences — the very embodiment of active, vigorous youth.

Wistful I said the eyes were, and yet they were not sad. Whatever thoughts lay hidden in that boy's mind — he was only ten years old, remember, — they were certainly not thoughts of melancholy or despair. " God tempers the wind to the shorn lamb," and " the back is fitted to the burthen," are phrases so common that we almost smile to repeat them or believe in them, and yet they are true. Any one whose enjoyments have been narrowed down by long sickness may prove their truth by recollecting how at last even the desire for impossible pleasures passes away. And in this case the deprivation was not sudden— the child had been born thus crippled, and had never been accustomed to any other sort of existence than this. What thoughts, speculations, or regrets might have passed through his mind, or whether he had as yet reflected upon his own condition at all, those about him could not judge. He was always a silent child, and latterly had grown more silent than ever. It was this silence, causing a fear lest the too rapidly developing mind might affect still more injuriously the imperfect and feeble body, which induced his guardian, counselled by Dr. Hamilton, to try a total change of life by sending him home to the shores of Loch Beg.

One thing certainly Mr. Cardross need not have dreaded — the child was no idiot. An intelligence, precocious to an almost painful extent, was visible in that poor little face — which seemed thirstingly to take in everything and to let nothing escape its observation.

The carriage drove slowly through the woods and along the shore of the loch — Mr. Menteith and Mrs. Campbell sitting opposite to the Earl; not noticing him much — even as a child he was sensitive of being watched — but making occasional comments on the scenery and other things.

"There is the kirk-tower; I mind it weel," said Mrs. Campbell, who still kept some accent of the clachan, though, like many Highlanders, she had it more in tone than in pronunciation, and often spoke almost pure English; which indeed she had taken pains to acquire, lest she might be transferred from her charge for fear of teaching him to speak as a young nobleman ought not to speak. But at sight of her native place some touch of the old tongue returned.

"That is the kirk, nurse, where my father and mother are buried?"

"Yes, my Lord."

"Will there be many people there? You know I never went to church but once before in all my life."

"Would ye like not to go now?

If so, I 'll turn back with ye this minute, my lamb — my Lord, I mean."

" No, thank you, nurse, I like to go. You know, Mr. Menteith promised me I should go about everywhere as soon as I came to live at Cairnforth."

" Everywhere you like, that is not too much trouble to your lordship," said Mr. Menteith, who was always tenaciously careful about the respect, of word and act, that he paid, and insisted should be paid, to his poor young ward.

" Oh, it 's no trouble to me, Malcolm takes care of that. And I like to see the world. If you and Dr. Hamilton would have let me, I think I would so have enjoyed going to school like other boys."

"Would you, my Lord?" answered Mr. Menteith, compassionately; but Mrs. Campbell who never could bear that pitying look and tone directed towards her nursling, said, a little sharply,—

"It's better as it is — dinna ye ken? Far mair fitting for his lordship's rank and position that he should get his learning all by himsel at his ain Castle, and with his ain tutor, and that sic a gentleman as Mr. Cardross ——"

"What is Mr. Cardross like?"

"Ye'll hear him preach the day."

"Will he teach me all by myself, as nurse says? Has he any children?— any boys, like me?"

"He has boys," said Mr. Menteith, avoiding more explicit information. For with a natural if mistaken precaution he had always kept his own sturdy, stalwart boys quite out of the way of the poor little Earl, and had especially cautioned the minister to do the same.

"I do long to play with boys. May I?"

"If you wish it, my Lord."

"And may I have a boat on that beautiful loch, and be rowed about just where I please? Malcolm says it would not shake me nearly so much as the carriage. May I go to the kirk every Sunday, and see everything and everybody, and read as many books as ever I choose? Oh, how happy I shall be! As happy as a king!"

" God help thee, my lamb ! " muttered Mrs. Campbell to herself — while even Mr. Menteith turned his face sedulously towards the loch and took snuff violently.

By this time they had reached the church - door, where the congregation were already gathering and hanging about, as Scotch congregations do, till service begins. But of this service, and this Sunday — which was so strangely momentous a day in more lives than one — the next chapter must tell.

Chapter the Third.

THE carriage of the Earl of Cairnforth, with its familiar and yet
long unfamiliar liveries, produced a keen
sensation among the simple folk who
formed the congregation of Cairnforth.
But they had too much habitual respect
for the great house and great folk of
the place, mingled with their national
shyness and independence, to stare very
much. A few moved aside to make
way for the two grand Edinburgh footmen, who leaped down from their perch

in order to render customary assistance to the occupants of the carriage.

Mrs. Campbell and Mr. Menteith descended first — and then the two footmen looked puzzled as to what they should do next.

But Malcolm was before them: Malcolm, who never suffered mortal man but himself to render the least assistance to his young master ; who watched and tended him ; waited on and fed him in the day, and slept in his room at night ; who, in truth, had now, for a year past, slipped into all the offices of a nurse as well as servant, and performed them with a woman's tenderness, care, and skill. Lord Cairnforth's eyes brightened when he saw him: and, carried in Malcolm's arms,—a few stragglers of the congregation standing aside to let them pass,—the young Earl was brought to the door of the kirk where his family had worshipped for generations.

Two elders stood there beside the plate — white-headed farmers, who remembered both the late Lord and the one before him.

"Yon's the Earl," whispered they, and came forward respectfully — then, startled by the unexpected and pitiful sight, they shrank back. But either the boy did not notice this, or was so used to it, that he showed no surprise.

"My purse, Malcolm," the small, soft voice was heard to say.

" Ay, my Lord. What will ye put into the plate ? "

" A guinea, I think, to-day, because I am so very happy."

This answer, which the two elders overheard, was told by them next day to everybody, and remembered along the loch-side for years.

Cairnforth Kirk, like most other Scotch churches of ancient date, is very plain within and without; and the congregation then consisted almost entirely of hill-side farmers, shepherds, and the like ; who arrived in families — dogs and all — for the dogs always came to church and behaved there as decorously as their masters. Many of the people walked eight, ten, and even twelve miles, from the extreme boundary of the parish; and waited about in the kirk or kirk-yard on fine Sundays, and in the Manse kitchen on wet ones—which were much the most frequent—during the two hours' interval between sermons.

In the whole congregation there was hardly a person above the labouring class, except in the minister's pew, and that belonging to the Castle; which had been newly lined and cushioned; and in a corner of which, safely deposited by Malcolm, the little Earl now sat. Sat always—even during the prayer—at which some of the congregation looked reprovingly round—but only saw the little figure wrapped in a plaid, and the sweet, wan, childish, and yet unchild-like face, with the curly dark hair and large dark eyes.

Whatever in the Earl was "no a' richt," it certainly could not be his mind; for a brighter, more intelligent countenance was never seen. It quite startled the minister with the intentness of its gaze, from the moment he ascended the pulpit; and though he tried not to look that way, and was very nervous, he could not get over the impression it made. It was to him almost like a face from the grave — this strange, eerie child's face, so strongly resembling that of the dead Countess, who, despite the difference in rank, had, during the brief year she lived and reigned at Cairnforth, been almost like an equal friend and companion to his own dead wife. Their two faces — Lady Cairnforth's as she looked the last time he saw her in her coffin — and his wife's as she lay in hers — mingled together, and affected him powerfully.

The good minister was not remarkable for the brilliancy of his sermons, which he wrote and " committed," that is, learnt by heart, to deliver in pseudo - extempore fashion, as was the weary custom of most Scotch ministers of his time. But this Sunday, all that he had committed slipped clean out of his memory. He preached, as he had never been known to preach before, and never preached again — with originality, power, eloquence : speaking from his deepest heart, as if the words thence pouring out had been supernaturally put into it : which, with a superstition that approached to sublimest faith, he afterwards solemnly believed they had been.

The text was that verse about " all things working together for good to them that love God ;"—but whatever the original discourse had been, it wandered off into a subject which all who knew the minister recognised as one perpetually close to his heart : submission to the will of God — whatever that will might be, and however incomprehensible it seemed to mortal eyes.

"Not, my friends," said he, after speaking for a long time on this head — speaking, rather than sermonizing, which, like many cultivated but not very original minds, he was too prone to do — " Not that I would encourage or excuse that weak yielding to calamity, which looks like submission, but is in fact only cowardice; submitting to all things as to a sort of fatality — without struggling against them, or trying to distinguish how much of them is the will of God, and how much our own weak will—daunted by the first shadow of misfortune. Especially misfortunes in our worldly affairs, wherein so much often happens for which we have ourselves only to blame. Submission to man is one thing — submission to God another. The latter is divine—the former is often merely contemptible. But even to the Almighty Father we should yield not a blind, crushed resignation, but an open-eyed obedience — like that we would fain win from our own children, desiring to make of them children, not slaves.

" My children, for I speak to the very youngest of you here, — and do try to understand me if you can, or as much as you can, — it is right — it is God's will — that you should resist, to the very last, any trial which is not inevitable. There are in this world countless sorrows, which, so far as appears, we actually bring on ourselves and others by our own folly, wickedness, or weakness — which is often as fatal as wickedness : and then we blame Providence for it, and sink into total despair. But when, as sometimes happens, His heavy hand is laid upon us in a visible, inevitable misfortune — which we cannot struggle against, and from which no human aid can save us, — then we ought to learn His hardest lesson — to submit. To submit — yet still, while saying ' Thy will be done,' to strive, so far as we can, *to do it.* If He have taken from us all but one talent, even that, my children, let us not bury in a napkin. Let us rather put it out at usury — leaving to Him to determine how much we shall receive again. For it is according to our use of what we have, and not of what we have not, that He will call us ' good and faithful servants,' and at last — when the long struggle of living shall be over — will bid us ' enter into the joy of our Lord.' "

When the minister sat down, he saw, as he had seen, consciously or unconsciously, all through the service, and above the entire congregation, those two large intent eyes fixed upon him from the Cairnforth pew.

Children of ten years old do not usually listen much to sermons, but the little Earl had heard very few, for it was difficult to take him to church without so many people staring at him. Nevertheless he listened to this sermon, so plain and clear, suited to the capacity of ignorant shepherds and little children, and seemed as if he understood it all. If he did not then, he did afterwards.

When service was over, he sat watching the congregation pass out, especially noticing a family of boys who occupied the adjoining pew. They had neither father nor mother with them, but an elder sister—as she appeared to be; a tall girl of about fifteen. She marshalled them out before her, not allowing them once to turn—as many of the other people did— to look with curiosity at the poor little Earl. But in quitting the kirk, she stopped at the vestry door, apparently to say a word to the minister; after which Mr. Cardross came forward, his gown over his arm, and spoke to Mr. Menteith,—

"Where is Lord Cairnforth? I was so glad to see him here."

"Thank you, Mr. Cardross," replied a weak, but cheerful voice from Malcolm's shoulder—which so startled the good minister, that he found not another word for a whole minute. At last he said, hesitating—

"Helen has just been reminding me

that the Earl and Countess used always to come and rest at the Manse between sermons. Would Lord Cairnforth like to do the same? It is a good way to the Castle—or perhaps he is too fatigued for the afternoon service?"

"Oh, no. I should like it very much. And, nurse, I do so want to see Mr. Cardross's children — and Helen. Who is Helen?"

"My daughter. Come here, Helen, and speak to the Earl."

She came forward—the tall girl who had sat at the end of the pew, in charge of the six boys: came forward in her serious, gentle, motherly way—alas! she was the only mother at the Manse now—and put out her hand—but instinctively drew it back again. For oh! what poor, helpless, unnatural-looking fingers were feebly advanced an inch or so to meet hers! They actually shocked her—gave her a sick sense of physical repulsion; but she conquered it. Then by a sudden impulse of conscience, quite forgetting the rank of the Earl, and only thinking of the poor, crippled, orphaned baby — for he seemed no more than a baby — Helen did what her warm, loving heart was in the habit of doing, as silent consolation for everything, to her own tribe of "mitherless bairns" — she stooped forward and kissed him.

The little Earl was so astonished that he blushed up to the very brow. But from that minute he loved Helen Cardross

—and never ceased loving her to the end of his days.

She led the way to the Manse, which was so close behind the kirk, that the back windows of it looked on the grave-yard. But in front there was a beautiful lawn and garden—the prettiest Manse garden that ever was seen. Helen stepped through it with her light, quick step, a child clinging to each hand—often turning round to speak to Malcolm, or to the Earl. He followed her with his eyes, and thought she was like a picture he had once seen of a guardian angel leading two children along. Though there was not a bit of the angel about Helen Cardross — externally, at least: she being one of those large, rosy, round-faced, flaxen-haired Scotch girls who are far from pretty, even in youth, and in middle age sometimes grow quite coarse and plain. She would not do so — and did not; for any body so good, so sweet, so bright, must always carry about with her, even to old age, something which, if not beauty's self, is beauty's atmosphere — and which often creates, even around unlovely people, a light and a glory as perfect as the atmosphere round the sun.

She took her seat—her poor mother's that used to be, at the head of the Manse-table; which was a little quieter on Sundays than week-days, and especially this Sunday, when the children were all awed and shy before their new visitor. Helen had previously taken them all aside, and explained to them that they were not to notice any thing in the Earl that was different from other people — that he was a poor little crippled boy who had neither father, mother, brother, nor sister; that they were to be very kind to him—but not to look at him much, and to make no remarks upon him on any account whatever.

And so, even though he was placed in baby's high chair, and fed by Malcolm almost as if he were a baby — he, who though no bigger than a baby, was in reality a boy of ten years old whom papa talked to, and who talked with papa almost as cleverly as Helen herself—still the Manse children were so well behaved that nothing occurred to make any body uncomfortable.

For the little Earl, he seemed to enjoy himself amazingly. He sat in his high chair, and looked round the well-filled table with mingled curiosity and amusement: inquired the children's names; and was greatly interested in the dog, the cat, a rabbit, and two kittens, which after dinner, they successively brought to amuse him. And then he invited them all to the Castle next day—and promised to take them over his garden there.

"But how can you take us?" said the youngest—in spite of Helen's frown—"We can run about—but you——"

"I can't run about, that is true. But I have a little carriage, and Malcolm draws it; or Malcolm carries me — and then I can see such a deal. I used to see nothing —only lie on a sofa all day—and have doctors coming about me and hurting me," added the poor little Earl, growing confidential, as one by one the boys slipped away, leaving him alone with Helen.

"Did they hurt you very much?" asked she.

"Oh, terribly. But I never told. You see, there was no use in telling; it could not be helped, and it would only have made nurse cry—she always cries over me. I think that is why I like Malcolm—he always helps me, and he never cries. And I am getting a great boy now: I was ten years old last week."

Ten years old—though he seemed scarcely more than five, except by the old look of his face. But Helen took no notice—only saying, "that she hoped the doctors did not hurt him now."

"No—that is all over. Dr. Hamilton says I am to be left to nature—whatever that is;—I overheard him say it one day. And I begged of Mr. Menteith not to shut me up any longer, or take me out only in my carriage—but to let me go about as I like, Malcolm carrying me—isn't he a big, strong fellow?—You can't think how nice it is to be carried about, and see every thing—oh! it makes me so happy!"

The tone in which he said "so happy"—made the tears start to Helen's eyes. She turned away to the window, where she saw her own big brothers, homely-featured and coarsely clad, but full of health, and strength, and activity—and then looked at this poor boy, who had every thing that fortune could give, and yet — nothing ! She thought how they grumbled and squabbled—those rough lads of hers — how she herself often felt the burthen of the large narrow household more than she could bear, and lost heart and temper. Then she thought of him — poor, helpless soul !—you could hardly say body —who could neither move hand nor foot— who was dependent as an infant on the kindness or compassion of those about him. Yet he talked of being " so happy ! " And there entered into Helen Cardross's good heart towards the Earl of Cairnforth a deep tenderness which, from that hour, nothing ever altered or estranged.

It was not pity — something far deeper. Had he been fretful, fractious, disagreeable

—she would still have been very sorry for him and very kind to him. But now, to see him as he was — cheerful, patient; so ready with his interest in others, so utterly without envyings and complainings regarding himself,— changed what would otherwise have been mere compassion, into actual reverence. As she sat beside him in his little chair, not looking at him much, for she still found it difficult to overcome the painful impression of the sight of that crippled and deformed body, she felt a choking in her throat and a dimness in her eyes — a longing to do any thing in the wide world that would help or comfort the poor little Earl.

"Do you learn any lessons?" asked she, thinking he seemed to enjoy talking with her. "I thought at dinner to-day that you seemed to know a great many things."

"Did I? That is very odd; for I fancied I knew nothing — and I want to learn every thing: if Mr. Cardross will teach me. I should like to sit and read all day long—I could do it by myself, now that I have found out a way of holding the book and turning over the leaves without nurse's helping me. Malcolm invented it — Malcolm is so clever and so kind."

"Is Malcolm always with you?"

"Oh, yes — how could I do without Malcolm? And you are quite sure your father will teach me every thing I want to learn?" pursued the little Earl, very eagerly.

Helen was quite sure.

"And there is another thing. Mr. Menteith says I must try, if possible, to learn to write—if only so as to be able to sign my name. In eleven more years, when I am a man, he says I shall often be required to sign my name. Do you think I could manage to learn?"

Helen looked at the poor, twisted, powerless fingers, and doubted it very much. Still she said cheerfully, "It would anyhow be a good thing to try."

"So it would—and I'll try. I'll begin to-morrow. Will you"—with a pathetic entreaty in the soft eyes—"it might be too much trouble for Mr. Cardross — but will *you* teach me?"

"Yes, my dear!" said Helen warmly. "That I will."

"Thank you! And"—still hesitating—"please would you always call me 'my dear' instead of 'my lord;' and might I call you Helen?"

So they "made a paction 'twixt them twa"—the poor, little, helpless, crippled boy, and the bright, active, energetic girl—the Earl's son and the minister's daughter: one of those pactions which grow out of an inner similitude which counteracts all outward dissimilarity; and they never broke it while they lived.

"Has my lamb enjoyed himself?" inquired Mrs. Campbell — anxiously and .

affectionately, when she reappeared from the Manse kitchen. Then, with a sudden resumption of dignity — "I beg your pardon, Miss Cardross, but this is the first time his lordship has ever been out to dinner."

"Oh, nurse—how I wish I might go out to dinner every Sunday! I am sure this has been the happiest day of all my life."

Chapter the Fourth.

F the "happiest day in all his life" had been the first day the Earl spent at Cairnforth Manse — which very likely it was,— he took the first possible opportunity of renewing his happiness.

Early on Monday forenoon,— while Helen's ever active hands were still busy clearing away the six empty porridge-plates, and the one tea-cup, which had contained the beverage which the minister loved, but which was too dear a luxury for any but the father of the family,—

Malcolm Campbell's large shadow was seen darkening the window.

"There's the Earl!" cried Helen — whose quick eye had already caught sight of the white little face, muffled up in Malcolm's plaid, and the soft black curls resting on his shoulder, damp with rain, and blown about by the wind — for it was what they called at Loch Beg a "coarse" day.

"My Lord was awfu' set upon coming," said Malcolm, apologetically — "And when my Lord taks a thing into his heid, he'll aye do't, ye ken."

"We are very glad to see the Earl," returned the minister, who, nevertheless, looked a little perplexed. For while finishing his breakfast he had been confiding to Helen how very nervous he felt about this morning's duties at the Castle — how painful it would be to teach a child so afflicted, and how he wished he had thought twice before he undertook the charge. And Helen had been trying to encourage him by telling him all that had passed between herself and the boy — how intelligent he had seemed, and how eager to learn. Still the very fact that they had been discussing him, made Mr. Cardross feel slightly confused. Men shrink so much more than women from any physical suffering or deformity: besides, except those few moments in the church, this was really the first time he had beheld Lord Cairnforth; for on

Sundays it was the minister's habit to pass the whole time between sermons in his study, and not join the family table until tea.

"We are very glad to see the Earl at all times," repeated he — but hesitatingly, as if not sure that he was quite speaking the truth.

"Yes, very glad," added Helen, hastily, fancying she could detect in the prematurely acute and sensitive face a consciousness that he was not altogether welcome. "My father was this minute preparing to start for the Castle."

"My Lord didna like to trouble the minister to be walking out this coarse day," said Malcolm, with true Highland ingenuity of politeness. "His Lordship thocht that instead o' Mr. Cardross coming to him, he would just come to Mr. Cardross."

"No, Malcolm," interposed the little voice, "it was not exactly that. I wished for my own sake to come to the Manse again—and to ask if I might come every day and take my lessons here—it's so dreary in that big library. I'll not be much trouble, indeed, sir," he added, entreatingly. "Malcolm will carry me in and carry me out—I can sit on almost any sort of chair now; and with this wee bit of stick in my hand I can turn over the leaves of my books my very own self—I assure you I can."

The minister walked to the window. He literally could not speak for a minute : he felt so deeply moved : and in his secret heart, so very much ashamed of himself.

When he turned round Malcolm had placed the little figure in an arm-chair by the fire, and was busy unswathing the voluminous folds of the plaid in which it had been wrapped. Helen, after a glance or two, pretended to be equally busy over her daily duty — the common duty of Scotch housewives at that period — of washing up the delicate china with her own neat hands, and putting it safe away in the parlour press. For, as before said, Mr. Cardross's income was very small — and, like that of most country ministers, very uncertain, his stipend altering, year by year, according to the price of corn. They kept one "lassie" to help — but Helen herself had to do a great deal of the housework. She went on doing it now; as probably she would in any case, being at once too simple and too proud to be ashamed of it: still she was glad to seem busy, lest the Earl might have fancied she was watching him.

Her feminine instinct had been right. Now, for the first time taken out of his shut-up nursery life, where he himself had been the principal object — where he had no playfellows, and no companions, save those he had been used to from infancy, — removed from this, and brought into ordinary family life, the poor child felt — he could not but feel — the sad, sad difference between himself and all the rest of the world. His colour came and went — he looked anxiously, deprecatingly, at Mr. Cardross.

" I hope, sir, you are not displeased with me for coming to-day. I shall not be very much trouble to you — at least I will try to be as little trouble as I can."

" My boy," said the minister — crossing over to him and laying his hand upon his head, "you will not be the least trouble. And if you were ever so much, I would cheerfully undertake it, for the sake of your father and mother — and —" he added, more to himself than aloud — "for your own."

That was true. Nature—which is never without her compensations — had put into this child of ten years old a strange charm, an inexpressible loveableness; that loveableness which springs from lovingness, though every loving nature is not fortunate enough to possess it. But the Earl's did; and as he looked up into the minister's face, with that touchingly grateful expression he had, the good man felt his heart melt and brim over at his eyes.

"You don't dislike me, then, because — because I am not like other boys?"

Mr. Cardross smiled, though his eyes were still dim, and his voice not clear; and with that smile vanished for ever the slight repulsion he had felt to the poor child; he took him permanently into his good heart—and from his manner the Earl at once knew that it was so.

He brightened up immediately.

"Now, Malcolm, carry me in; I 'm quite ready," said he, in a tone which indicated that quality, discernible even at so early an age — a "will of his own." To see the way he ordered Malcolm about — the big fellow obeying him, with something beyond even the large limits of that feudal respect which his forbears had paid to the Earl's forbears for many a generation — was a sight at once touching and hopeful.

"There — put me into the child's chair I had at dinner yesterday. Now, fetch me a pillow — or rather roll up your plaid into one — don't trouble Miss Cardross. That will make me quite comfortable. Pull out my books from your pouch, Malcolm, and spread them out on the table: and then go and have a crack with your old friends at the clachan — you can come for me in two hours."

It was strange to see the little figure giving its orders, and settling itself with the preciseness of an old man at the study-table; but still this removed somewhat of the painful shyness and uncomfortableness from everybody, and especially from Mr. Cardross. He seated himself in his familiar arm-chair, and looked across the table at his poor little pupil, who seemed at once so helpless and so strong.

Lessons began. The child was exceedingly intelligent, precociously,—nay, preternaturally so, it appeared to Mr. Cardross, who, like many another learned father, had been blessed with rather stupid boys, who liked anything better than study, and whom he had with great labour dragged through a course of ordinary English, Latin, and even a fragment of Greek. But this boy seemed all brains. His cheeks flushed, his eyes glittered, he learnt as if he actually enjoyed learning. True, as Mr. Cardross soon discovered, his acquirements were not at all in the regular routine of education: he was greatly at fault in many simple things; but the amount of heterogeneous and out-of-the-way knowledge which he had gathered up, from all available sources, was quite marvellous.—And above all, to teach a boy unto whom learning seemed a pleasure rather than a torment, a favour instead of a punishment, was such an exceeding and novel delight to the good minister, that soon he forgot the crippled figure — the helpless hands that sometimes with fingers, sometimes even with teeth, painfully guided the ingeniously cut forked stick, and the thin face that only too often turned white and weary, but quickly looked up, as if struggling against weakness, and concentrating all attention on the work that was to be done.

At twelve o'clock Helen came in with her father's lunch — a foaming glass of new milk, warm from the cow. The little Earl looked at it with eager eyes.

"Will I bring you one too?" said Helen.

"Oh — thank you ; I am so thirsty. And please — would you move me a little — just a very little : I don't often sit so long in one position. It won't trouble you very much, will it ? "

"Not at all — if you will only show me how," — stammered Helen, turning hot and red. But shaking off her hesitation, she lifted up the poor child, tenderly and carefully — shook his pillows and " sorted " him according to her own untranslateable Scotch word ; then went quickly out of the room to compose herself, for she had done it all, trembling exceedingly the while. And yet, somehow, a feeling of great tenderness — tenderer than even that she had felt successively towards her own baby brothers, had grown up in her heart towards him — taking away every possible feeling of repulsion on account of his deformity.

She brought back the glass of creamy milk and a bit of oatcake, and laid them beside the Earl. He regarded them wistfully.

"How nice the milk looks! I am so tired — and so thirsty. Please, — would you give me some? Just hold the glass, that's all — and I can manage."

Helen held it to his lips — the first time she ever did so; but not the last by many. Years and years from then — when she herself was quite an old woman, she remembered giving him that drink of milk — and how, afterwards, two large soft eyes were turned upon hers, so lovingly, so gratefully, as if the poor cripple had drunk in something besides milk — the sweet draught of human affection, not dried up even to such heavily afflicted ones as he.

"Are lessons all done for to-day, papa?" said she, noticing that, eager as it was, the little face looked very wan and wearied; but also noticing with delight, that her father's expression was brighter and more interested than it had been this long time.

"Done, Helen? Well, if my pupil is tired — certainly."

"But I'm not tired, sir."

Helen shook her motherly head. "Quite enough for to-day. You may come back again to-morrow."

He did come back. Day after day, in fair weather or foul, big Malcolm was to be seen stepping, with his free Highland step — Malcolm was a lissome, handsome young fellow — across the Manse garden, carrying that small, frail burthen, which all the inhabitants of the clachan had ceased to stare at, and to which they all raised their bonnets or touched their shaggy forelocks. — " It's the wee Earl, ye ken," — and once and all treated with the utmost respect the tiny figure wrapped in a plaid, so that nothing was visible except a small child's face — which always smiled at sight of other children.

It was surprising in how few days the clachan, and indeed the whole neighbourhood, grew accustomed to the appearance of the Earl, and his sad story. Perhaps this was partly due to Helen and Mr. Cardross, who, seeing no longer any occasion for mystery, indeed regretting a little that any mystery had ever been made about the matter, took every opportunity of telling everybody who inquired the whole facts of the case.

These were few enough — and simple enough, though very sad. The Earl—the last Earl of Cairnforth — was a hopeless cripple for life. All the consultations of all the doctors had resulted in that conclusion. It was very unlikely he would ever be better than he was now—physically; but mentally, he was certainly "a' richt," — or "a' there," — as the country-folk express it. There was, as Mr. Cardross carefully explained to everybody, not the slightest ground for supposing him deficient in intellect: on the contrary, his intellect seemed almost painfully acute. The quickness with which he learned his lessons, surpassed that of any boy of his age the minister had ever known; and he noticed every thing around him so closely, and made such intelligent remarks, that to talk with him was like talking with a grown man. Before the first week was over, Mr. Cardross began actually to enjoy the child's company, and to look forward to lesson hours as the pleasantest hours of his day. For since the Castle was closed the minister's lot had been the almost inevitable lot of a country clergyman; whose parish contains many excellent people, who look up to him with the utmost reverence, and for whom he entertains the sincere respect that worth must always feel towards worth, but with whom he had very few intellectual sympathies. In truth, since Mrs. Cardross died the minister had shut himself up almost entirely; and had scarcely had a single interest out of his own study — until the Earl came home to Cairnforth.

Now, after lessons, he would occasionally be persuaded to quit that beloved study, and take a walk along the loch side, or across the moor, to show his pupil the country of which he, poor little fellow, was owner and lord. He did it at first out of pure kindness, to save the Earl from the well-meant intrusion of neighbours, but afterwards from sheer pleasure in seeing the boy so happy. To him, mounted in Malcolm's arms, and brought for the first time into contact with the outer world, every thing was a novelty and delight. And his quick perception let nothing escape him. He seemed to watch lovingly all nature; from the grand lights and shadows which moved over the mountains, to the little moorland flowers which he made Malcolm stop to gather. All living things too: from the young rabbit that scudded across their path, to the lark that rose singing up into the wide blue air — he saw and noticed every thing.

But he never once said — what Helen, who, as often as her house duties allowed, delighted to accompany them on these expeditions, was always expecting he would say — why had God given these soulless creatures legs to run and wings to fly, strength, health, and activity to enjoy existence, and denied all these things to him? Denied them, not for a week, a month, a year, but for his whole lifetime — a lifetime so short at best; — "few of days, and full of trouble." Why could He not have made it a little more happy?

Thousands have asked themselves, in some form or other, the same unanswered, unanswerable question. Helen had done so already, young as she was; when her mother died, and her father seemed slowly breaking down, and the whole world appeared to her full of darkness and woe. How then must it have appeared to this poor boy? But, strange to say, that bitter doubt, which so often came into Helen's heart, never fell from the child's lips at all. Either he was still a mere child, accepting life just as he saw it, and seeking no solution of its mysteries; or else, though so young, he was still strong enough to keep his doubts to himself, to bear his own burthen, and trouble no one.

Or else — and when she watched his inexpressibly sweet face, which had the look you sometimes see in blind faces, of absolutely untroubled peace, Helen was forced to believe this — God, who had taken away from him so much, had given him something still more:—a spiritual insight so deep and clear, that he was happy in spite of his heavy misfortune. She never looked at him, but she thought involuntarily of the text, out of the only book with which unlearned Helen was very familiar —that "in heaven, their angels do always behold the face of my Father which is in heaven."

After a fortnight's stay at the Castle, Mr. Menteith felt convinced that his experiment had succeeded—and that, onerrous as the duty of guardian was, he might be satisfied to leave his ward under the charge of Mr. Cardross.

"Only, if those Bruces should try to get at him, you must let me know at once. Remember, I trust you."

"Certainly you may. Has any thing been heard of them lately?"

"Not much: beyond the continual applications for advances of the annual sum which the late Earl gave them; and which I continue to pay — just to keep them out of the way."

"They are still abroad?"

"I suppose so. But I hear very little about them. They were relations on the Countess's side, you know — it was she who brought the money. Poor little fellow — what an accumulation it will be by the time he is of age, and what small good it will do him!"

And the honest man sighed as he looked from Mr. Cardross's dining-room window across the Manse garden, where, under a shady tree, was placed the Earl's little wheel-chair, which was an occasional substitute for Malcolm's arms. In it he sat, with a book on his lap, and with that aspect of entire content which was so very touching. Helen sat beside him on the grass, sewing — she was always sewing; and indeed she had need, if her needle were to keep pace with its requirements in that large family of boys.

"That's a good girl of yours, and his lordship seems to have taken to her amazingly. I am very glad, for he had no feminine company at all except Mrs. Campbell, and good as she is, she isn't quite the thing — not exactly a lady, you see. Eh, Mr. Cardross — what a lady his mother was! We'll never again see the like of the poor Countess. Nor in all human probability, shall we ever again see another Countess of Cairnforth."

"No."

"Yet," continued Mr. Menteith, after a long pause — "Dr. Hamilton thinks he may live many years. Strange to say, his constitution is healthy and sound — and his sweet, placid nature — his mother's own nature (isn't he very like her sometimes?) — gives him so much advantage in struggling through every ailment. If he can be made happy, — as you and Helen will, I doubt not, be able to make him, and kept strictly to a wholesome, natural country life here, it is not impossible he may live to enter upon his property. And then — for the future, God knows!"

"It is well for us," replied the

minister gravely — "that He does know — every thing."

"I suppose it is."

And then for another hour the two good men — one living in the world and the other out of it — both fathers of families, carrying their own burthen of cares, and having gone through their own personal sorrows, each in his day — talked over, in the minutest degree, the present, and so far as they could divine it, the future of this poor boy, who, through so strange a combination of circumstances, had been left entirely to their charge.

"It is a most responsible charge, Mr. Cardross, and I feel almost selfish in shifting it so much from my own shoulders upon yours."

"I am willing to undertake it. Perhaps it may do me good," returned the minister, with a slight sigh.

"And you will give him the best education you can — your own, in short, which is more than sufficient for any Lord Cairnforth: certainly more than the last Earl had, or his father either."

"Possibly," said Mr. Cardross, who remembered both — stalwart, active, courtly lords of the soil, great at field-sports and festivities, but not over-given to study. "No, the present Earl does not take after his progenitors in any way. You should just see him, Mr. Menteith, over his Virgil; and I have promised to begin Homer with him to-morrow. It does one's heart good to see a boy so fond of his books," added the minister, warming up into an enthusiasm which delighted the other extremely.

"Yes — I think my plan was right," said he, rubbing his hands. "It will work well on both sides. There could not be found anywhere a better tutor than yourself for the Earl. He never can go much into the world — he may not even live to be of age: still, as long as he does live, his life ought to be made as pleasant — I mean as little pain-ful — to him as possible. And he ought to be fitted, in case he should live, for as many as he can fulfil of the duties of his position: its enjoyments, alas! he will never know."

"I am not so sure of that," replied

Mr. Cardross. "He loves books: he may turn out a thoroughly educated and accomplished student: perhaps even a man of letters. To have a thirst for knowledge, and unlimited means to gratify it, is not such a bad thing. Why," continued the minister, glancing round on his own poorly furnished shelves, where every book was bought almost at the sacrifice of a meal — " he will be rich enough to stock from end to end that wilderness of shelves in the half-finished Castle library. How pleasant that must be!"

Mr. Menteith smiled, as if he did not quite comprehend this sort of felicity. "But in any case, Lord Cairnforth seems to have, what will be quite as useful to him as brains — a very kindly heart. He does not shut himself up in a morbid way, but takes an interest in all about him. Look at him, now, how heartily he is laughing at something your daughter has said. Really, these two seem quite happy."

"Helen makes everybody happy," fondly said Helen's father.

"I believe so. I shall be sending down one of my big lads to look after her some day. I've eight of them, Mr. Cardross — all to be educated, settled, and wived. It's a 'sair fecht,' I assure you."

"I know it. But still it has its compensations."

" Ay, they're all strong, likely, braw fellows, who can push their own way in the world and fend for themselves. Not like —" he glanced over to the group on the grass, and stopped. Yet, at that moment a hearty trill of thoroughly childish laughter seemed to rebuke the regrets of both fathers.

" That child certainly has the sweetest nature — the most remarkable faculty for enjoying other people's enjoyments, in which he himself can never share."

" Yes, it was always so, from the time he was a mere infant. Dr. Hamilton often noticed it, and said it was a good omen."

" I believe so," rejoined Mr. Cardross, earnestly. " I feel sure that if Lord

Cairnforth lives, he will neither have a useless nor an unhappy life."

" Let us hope not. And yet, poor little fellow! — To be the last Earl of Cairnforth — and to be — such as he is ! "

" He is what God made him, what God willed him to be," said the minister, solemnly. " We know not why it should be so: we only know that it is — and we cannot alter it. We cannot remove from him his heavy cross; but I think we can help him to bear it."

" You are a good man, Mr. Cardross," replied the Edinburgh writer, huskily, as he rose from his seat — and declining another glass of the claret, of which, under some shallow pretext, he had sent a supply into the minister's empty cellar— he crossed the grass-plot, and spent the rest of the evening beside his ward and Helen.

Chapter the Fifth.

AYS, months, and years, slip smoothly by on the shores of Loch Beg. Even now, though the cruelly advancing finger of Civilization has touched it, dotted it with genteel villas on either side, ploughed it with smoky steam-boats, and will shortly frighten the innocent fishes by dropping a marine telegraph wire across the mouth of the loch, it is a peaceful place still. But when the last Earl of Cairnforth was a child it was all peace. In summer time a few stray tourists would wander past it — wondering at its beauty; but in winter it had hardly any communication with the outer world. The Manse, the Castle, and the clachan, with a few outlying farm-houses, comprised the whole of Cairnforth; and the little peninsula, surrounded on three sides by water, and on the fourth by hills, was sufficiently impregnable and isolated to cause existence to flow on there very quietly, in what townspeople call dulness, and country people repose.

For whatever repose there may be in country life — real country, — there is certainly no monotony. The perpetual change of seasons, varying the aspect of the outside world every month, every week, — nay, almost every day, is a continual interest to observant minds. And especially so to intelligent children, who are, as yet, lying on the breast of Mother Nature only—nor have begun to feel or understand the darker and sadder interests of human passion and emotion.

The little Earl of Cairnforth was one of these; and many a time, through all the summers of his life, he recalled tenderly that first summer at Cairnforth, when, no longer pent up between walls and roofs, or dragged about in carriages, he learned, by Malcolm's aid, and under Helen's teaching, to chronicle time in different ways. First, by the hyacinths and primroses vanishing, and giving place to the wild roses — those exquisite deep-red roses which belong especially to this country-side; then, by the woods — his own woods, growing fragrant with innumerable honey-suckles; and, lastly, by the heather on the moorland — Scotland's own flower — which clothes entire hill-sides as with a garment of gorgeous purple, and fills the whole atmosphere with the scent of a spice-garden. And when it faded into a soft brown — dying delicately, beautiful to the last — there appeared the brambles, trailing everywhere, with their pretty yellowing leaves and their delicious berries. How blithe, even like a mere "callant," big Malcolm was, when, leaving the Earl on the sunny hill-side under Miss Cardross's charge, he used to wander off, and come back, with his hands all torn and scratched, to feed his young master with blackberries!

" He is not unhappy — I am sure the child is not unhappy," Helen often said to her father, when — as was his way — Mr. Cardross would fall into fits of uncertainty and downheartedness, and think he was killing his pupil with study, or wearying him, and risking his health by letting him do as much as his energetic mind, always dominant over the frail body, prompted him to do. " Only let him love his life, and put as much in it as he can, be it long or short, and then it will never be a sad life or a life thrown away."

" Helen, you 're not clever, but you 're a wise little woman, my dear," the minister would say, patting the flaxen curls, or the busy hands — large and brown, yet with a certain grace about them, too: helpful hands, made to hold children, or tend sick folk, or sustain the feeble steps of old age. She was " no bonnie," Helen Cardross; it was just a round, rosy, sonsie face, with no features in particular, but she was pleasant to look upon — and inexpressibly pleasant to live with. For it was such a wholesome nature; so entirely free from moods, or fancies, or crotchets of any kind — those sad vagaries of ill-health, ill-humour, and ill-conditionedness of every sort, which are sometimes only a misfortune caused by an unhappy natural temperament, but oftener arise from pure egotism — of which there was not an atom in Helen Cardross. Her life was like the life of a flower — as natural, unconscious, fresh and sweet: she took in every influence about her, and gave out freely all she had to give: desired no better things than she possessed, and where she was planted there she grew.

It was not wonderful that the little Earl loved her; and that under her sunshiny soul, his life, too, blossomed out as it might never otherwise have done, but have drooped and faded, and gone back into the darkness, imperfect and unfulfilled. For though each human life is, in a sense, complete to itself, and must work itself out independently, clinging to no other, still there is a great and beautiful mystery in the way one life seems to influence another; sometimes for ill, but far, far oftener for good.

Lord Cairnforth was not much with the Cardross boys. He liked them, and evidently craved after their company; but they were very shy of him. Sometimes they let Malcolm bring him into their boat, and condescended to row him up and down the loch — a mode of locomotion in which he greatly delighted. For, at best, the shaking of the great lumbering coach was not easy to him — and he always begged to be carried in Malcolm's arms — till he found how pleasantly he could lie in the stern of the

Manse boat, and float about on the smooth water, watching the mountains and the shores.

True, he could not stir an inch from where he was laid down; but he lay there so contentedly, enjoying everything, and really looked, what he often said he was, " as happy as a king."

And by degrees, with a little home persuasion from Helen, the boys got reconciled to his company: found, indeed, that he was not such bad company after all. For, often, when they were tired of pulling, and let the boat drift into some quiet, little bay, or rock lazily in the middle of the loch, the little Earl would begin talking — telling stories, which soon caught the attention of the minister's boys.

These were either fragments out of the books he had read — which seemed count-less to the young Cardrosses : or, what they liked still better, tales " out of his own head." And these tales were always the last that they would have expected from one like him : wild exploits ; wanderings over South American prairies, or shipwrecks on desert islands ; astonishing feats of riding, or fighting, or travelling by land and sea ; every thing, in short, belonging to that sort of active, energetic, adventurous life of which the relator could never have had the least experience, and never would have in this world. Perhaps for that very reason his fancy delighted therein the more.

And his stories were enjoyed by others as

much as by himself, which no doubt added to the charm of them. When winter came, and all the boating days were done, many a night, round the fire of the Manse parlour, or in the "awful eerie" library at the Castle, the Earl used to have a whole circle of young people, and some elder ones, too, gathered round his wheel-chair, listening to his wonderful tales of adventure by flood and field.

"Why don't you write them out properly?" the boys would ask sometimes; forgetting — what Helen would never have forgotten. But the Earl only looked down on his poor helpless fingers, and smiled.

However, he had, with great difficulty and pains, managed to learn to write, that is, to sign his name, or indite any short letter to Mr. Menteith or others; which, as he grew older, sometimes became necessary. But writing was always a great trouble to him; and fortunately, people were not expected to write much in those days. Had he been born a little later in his century, the Earl of Cairnforth might have brightened his sad life by putting his imagination forth in print, and becoming a great literary character: as it was, he merely told his tales for his own delight and that of those about him — which possibly was a better thing than fame.

Then he made jokes, too. Sometimes, in his quiet, dry way, he said such droll things that the Cardross boys fell into shouts of laughter. He had the rare quality of seeing the comical side of things, without a particle of ill-nature being mixed up with his fun. His wit danced about as brilliantly and harmlessly as the Northern lights that flashed and flamed of winter nights over the mountains at the head of the loch; and the solid, somewhat heavy Manse boys, gradually growing up to men, often wondered why it was that, miserable as the Earl's life was, or seemed to them, they always felt merrier, instead of sadder, when they were in his company.

But sometimes, when with Helen alone — and more especially as he grew to be a youth in his teens, and yet no bigger, no stronger, and scarcely less helpless than a child,— the young Earl would let fall a

word or two which showed that he was
fully and painfully aware of his own condition, and of all that it entailed. It was
evident that he had thought much and
deeply of the future which lay before him.
If, as now appeared probable, he should
live to man's estate, his life must, at
best, be one long endurance, rendered all
the sharper and harder to bear, because
within that helpless body dwelt a soul
which was, more than that of most men,
alive to everything beautiful, noble, active,
and good.

However, though he occasionally betrayed
these workings of his mind, it was only
to Helen, and not to her very much, for
he was exceedingly self-contained from
his very childhood. He seemed to feel

by instinct that to him had been allotted a special solitude of existence — into which, try as tenderly as they would, none could ever fully penetrate, and with which none could wholly sympathise. It was inevitable, in the nature of things. He apparently accepted the fact as such, and did not attempt to break through it. He took the strongest interest in other people, and in everything around him; but he did not seem to expect to have the like returned in any great degree. Perhaps it was one of those merciful compensations, that what he could not have he was made strong enough to do without.

So things went on, without any other variety than an occasional visit from Mr. Menteith or Dr. Hamilton, for seven years, during which the minister's pupil had acquired every possible learning that his teacher could give, and was fast becoming less a scholar than an equal companion and friend. So familiar and dear, that Mr. Cardross, like all who knew him, had long since almost forgotten that the Earl was — what he was. It seemed the most natural thing in the world that he should sit there in his little chair, doing nothing; absolutely passive to all physical things, but interested in everything and everybody, and, whether at the Manse or the Castle, as completely one of the circle as if he took the most active part therein. Consulted by one, appealed to by another, joked by a third — he was ever ready with a joke — it was only when strangers happened to see him, and were startled by the sight, that his own immediate friends recognised how different he was from other people.

It was one day, when he was about nineteen, that Helen, coming in to see him, with a message from her father, who wanted to speak to him about some parish matters, found Lord Cairnforth deeply meditating over a letter. He slipped it aside, however ; and it was not until the whole parish question had been discussed and settled, as somehow he and Helen very often did settle the whole affairs of the parish between them, that he brought it out again, fidgetting it out of his pocket with his poor fingers, which seemed a little more helpless than usual.

" Helen, I wish you would read that, and tell me what you think about it ? "

It was a letter somewhat painful to read, with the Earl sitting by and watching her, but Helen had long learnt never to shrink from these sort of things. He felt them far less, if everybody else faced them as boldly as he had himself always done.

The letter was from Dr. Hamilton — written after his return from a three days' visit at Cairnforth Castle. It explained, after a long apologetic preamble — the burthen of which was that the Earl was now old enough and thoughtful enough to be the best person to speak to on such a difficult subject — that there had been a certain skilful mechanician lately in Edinburgh, who declared he would invent some support by which Lord Cairnforth could be made — not indeed to walk, that was impossible — but to be by many degrees more active than now. But it would be necessary for him to go to London, and there submit to a great amount of trouble and inconvenience — possibly some pain.

"I tell you this last, my dear Lord," continued the good doctor, "because I ought not to deceive you; and because, so far as I have seen, you are a courageous boy — nay almost a man — or will be soon. I must forewarn you also that the experiment is only an experiment, that it may fail; but even in that case you would be only where you were before — no better, no worse — except for the temporary annoyance and suffering."

"And if it succeeded?" said Helen, almost in a whisper, as she returned the letter.

The Earl smiled — a bright, vague, but hopeful smile — "I might be a little more able to do things; to live my life with a little less trouble to myself, and possibly to other people. Well, Helen? You don't speak — but I think your eyes say 'try!'"

"Yes, my dear." She sometimes—though not often now, lest it might vex him by making him still so much of a child — called him " my dear."

This ended the conversation, which Helen did not communicate to any body, nor referred to again with Lord Cairnforth, though she pondered over it, and him, continually.

A week after this, Mr. Menteith unexpectedly appeared at the Castle, and after a long consultation with Mr. Cardross, it was agreed that what seemed the evident wish of the Earl should be accomplished, if possible; that he, Malcolm, Mrs. Campbell, and Mr. Menteith should start for London immediately.

Such a journey was then a very different thing from what it is now; and to so helpless a traveller as Lord Cairnforth its difficulties were doubled. He had to post the whole distance in his own carriage, which was fitted up so as to be as easy as possible in locomotion — besides being so arranged that he could sleep in it, if absolutely necessary; for ordinary beds and ordinary chairs were sometimes very painful to him. Had he been born poor, in all probability he would long ago have died — of sheer suffering.

Fortunately it was summer time: he stayed at Cairnforth till after his birthday, "for I may never see another," said he, with that gentle smile which seemed to imply that he would be neither glad nor sorry;—and then he started. He was quite cheerful himself; but Mr. Menteith and Mrs. Campbell looked very anxious. Malcolm was full of superstitious forebodings, and Helen Cardross and her father, when they bade him good-bye, and watched the carriage drive slowly from the Castle doors, felt as sad as if they were parting from him, not for London, but for the other world.

Not until he was gone did they recognise how much they missed him: in the Manse parlour, where "the Earl's chair" took its regular place — in the pretty Manse garden, where its wheels had made in the gravel walks deep marks which Helen could not bear to have erased,— in his pew at the kirk, where the minister had learnt to look Sunday after Sunday for that earnest, listening face. Mr. Cardross, too, found it dull no longer to have his walk up to the Castle, and his hour or two's rest in the yet unfinished library — which he and Lord Cairnforth had already begun to consult about, and where the Earl was always to be found, sitting at his little table with his books about him, and Malcolm lurking within call — or else placed contentedly by the French window, looking out upon that blaze of beauty into which the Countess's flower-garden had grown. How little they had thought — the young father and mother, cut off in the midst of their plans, that their poor child would one day so keenly enjoy them all, and have such sore need for these or any other simple and innocent enjoyments.

"Papa, how we do miss him!" said Helen one day as she walked with her father through the Cairnforth woods.

"Who would have thought it when he first came here, only a few years ago?"

"Who would indeed?" said the minister, remembering a certain walk he had taken through these very paths nineteen years before — when he had wondered why Providence had sent the poor babe into the world at all, and thought how far, far happier it would have been, lying dead on its dead mother's bosom; — that beautiful young mother, whose placid face upon the white satin pillows of her coffin, Mr. Cardross yet vividly recalled — for he saw it often reflected in the living face of the son whom, happily, she had died without beholding.

"That was a wise saying of King

David's — Let me fall into the hands of the Lord, and not into the hands of men," mused Mr. Cardross, who had just been hearing from Mr. Menteith a long story of his perplexities with "those Bruces," and had also had lately a few domestic dissensions among his own parishioners — who did quarrel among themselves occasionally, and always brought their quarrels to be settled by the minister. "It is a strange thing, Helen my dear, what wonderful peace there often is in great misfortunes. They are quite different from the petty miseries which people make for themselves."

"I suppose so. But do you think, papa, that any good will come out of this London journey?"

"I cannot tell. Still, it was right to try. You yourself said it was right to try."

"Yes," and then seeing it was done now — the practical, brave Helen stilled her uncertainties, and let the matter rest.

No one was surprised that weeks elapsed before there came any tidings of the travellers. Then Mr. Menteith wrote, announcing their safe arrival in London, which diffused great joy throughout the parish ; for of course every body knew whither Lord Cairnforth had gone, and many knew the reason why. Scarcely a week passed that some of the far distant tenantry even, who lived on the other side of the peninsula, did not cross the hills, walking many miles for no reason but to ask at the Manse what was the latest news of " our Earl."

But after the first letter there came no further tidings, and indeed none were expected. Mr. Menteith had probably returned to Edinburgh, and in those days there was no penny post, and nobody indulged in unnecessary correspondence. Still, sometimes Helen thought, with a sore uneasiness,, " If the Earl had had good news to tell, he would have surely told it. He was always so glad to make anybody happy."

The long summer twilights were ended, and one or two equinoctial gales had whipped the waters of Loch Beg into wild " white horses,"— yet still Lord Cairnforth did not return. At last, one Monday night, when Helen and her father were returning from a three days' absence at the "preachings" — that is, the half-yearly sacrament — in a neighbouring parish — they saw, when they came to the ferry, the glimmer of lights from the Castle windows on the opposite shore of the loch.

"I do believe Lord Cairnforth is come home!"

"Ou ay, Miss Helen," — said Duncan the ferryman. "His lordship crossed wi' me the day; an' I'm thinking, minister," added the old man, confidentially, "that ye suld just gang up to the Castle an' see him. For it's ma opinion that the Earl's come back as he gaed awa — nae better, and nae waur."

"What makes you think so? Did he say any thing?"

"Ne'er a word but just 'How are ye the day, Duncan?' and he sat and glowered at the hills and the loch — and twa big draps rolled down his puir bit facie — it's grown sae white and sae sma', ye ken — and I said, 'My lord, it's grand to see your lordship back. Ye'll no be gaun to London again, I hope?' 'Na, na,' says he — 'Na, Duncan — I'm best at hame — best at hame!' And when Malcolm lifted him, he gied a bit skreigh, as if he'd hurted himsel — Minister, I wish I'd thae London doctors here, by our loch side," muttered Duncan between his teeth, and pulling away fiercely at his oar; but the minister said nothing.

He and Helen went silently home; and finding no message, walked on as silently up to the Castle together.

Chapter the Sixth.

Chapter the Sixth.

OLD Duncan's penetration had been correct — the difficult and painful London journey was all in vain. Lord Cairnforth had returned home neither better nor worse than he was before — the experiment had failed.

Helen and her father guessed this from their first sight of him; though they had found him sitting as usual in his arm-chair at his favourite corner; and when they entered the library he had looked up with a smile — the same old smile, as natural as though he had never been away.

"Is that you, Mr. Cardross? Helen, too?—How very kind of you to come and see me so soon!"

But in spite of his cheerful greeting, they detected at once the expression of suffering in the poor face—"sae white and sae sma'," as Duncan had said: pale beyond its ordinary pallor, and shrunken and withered like an old man's. The more so, perhaps, as the masculine down had grown upon cheek and chin; and there was a matured manliness of expression in the whole countenance, which formed a strange contrast to the still puny and childish frame—alas, not a whit less help-less, or less distorted than before! Yes— the experiment had failed.

They were so sure of this, Mr. Cardross

and his daughter, that neither put to him a single question on the subject, but instinctively passed it over, and kept the conversation to all sorts of common-place topics: the journey, — the wonders of London, — and the small events which had happened in quiet Cairnforth during the three months that the Earl had been away.

Lord Cairnforth was the first to end their difficulty and hesitation by openly referring to that which neither of his friends could bear to speak of.

"Yes," he said, at last, with a faint, sad smile, "I agree with old Duncan: I never mean to go to London any more. I shall stay for the rest of my days among my own people."

"So much the better for them," observed the minister, warmly.

" Do you think that? Well, we shall see. I must try and make it so, as well as I can. I am but where I was before, as Dr. Hamilton said. Poor Dr. Hamilton! —he is so sorry."

Mr. Cardross did not ask about what— but turned to the table and began cutting open the leaves of a book. For Helen, she drew nearer to Lord Cairnforth's chair, and laid over the poor, weak, wasted fingers her soft, warm hand.

The tears sprang to the young Earl's eyes. "Don't speak to me," he whispered, "it is all over now; but it was very hard for a time."

" I know it."

" Yes — at least as much as you can know."

Helen was silent. She recognised, as she had never recognised before, the awful individuality of suffering which it had pleased God to lay upon this one human being — suffering, at which even the friends who loved him best could only stand aloof and gaze, without the possibility of alleviation.

" Ay," he said, at last, "it is all over —I need try no more experiments. I shall just sit still and be content."

What was the minute history of the experiments he had tried, how much bodily pain they had cost him, and through how much mental pain he had struggled, before he attained that "content," he did not explain even to Helen. He turned the conversation to the books which Mr. Cardross was cutting, and many other books — of which he had bought a whole cart-load for the minister's library. Neither then, nor at any other time, did he ever refer, except in the most cursory way, to his journey to London.

But Helen noticed that for a long while, weeks, — nay, months, he seemed to avoid more than ever any conversation about himself: he was slightly irritable and uncertain of mood, and disposed to shut himself up in the Castle — reading, or seeming to read, from morning till night. It was not till a passing illness of the minister's in some degree forced him, that he reappeared at the Manse, and fell into his old ways of coming and going, resuming his studies with Mr. Cardross, and his walks with Helen — or rather drives — for he had ceased to be carried in Malcolm's arms.

"I am a man now, or ought to be," he said once, as a reason for this: after which no one made any remarks on the subject. Malcolm still retained his place as the Earl's close attendant — as faithful as his shadow, almost as silent.

But the next year or so made a considerable alteration in Lord Cairnforth. Not in growth: the little figure never grew any bigger than that of a boy of ten or twelve; but the childish softness passed from the face; it sharpened, and hardened, and became that of a young

man.   The   features   developed;   and   a
short   black   beard,   soft   and   curly,   for   it
had   never   known   the   razor,   added   character   to   what,   in   ordinary   men,   would
have   been   considered   a   very   handsome   face.
It   had   none   of   the   painful   expression   so
often   seen   in   deformed   persons;   but   more
resembled   those   sweet   Italian   heads   of
youthful   saints — Saint   Sebastian's,   for   instance — which   the   old   masters   were   so
fond   of   painting.   And   though   there   was
a   certain   melancholy   about   it   when   in
repose,   during   conversation   it   brightened
up,   and   was   the   cheerfulest,   most   sunshiny
face   imaginable.

That   is — it   ultimately   became   so :   but
for   a   long   time   after   the   journey   to
London   a   shadow   hung   over   it,   which

hunting, shooting, fishing, and boating —
was impossible to this Earl. His distant
dependants hardly remembered his existence,
and he took no heed of theirs — until a
few months before he came of age, when
one of these slight chances which often
determine so much, changed the current of
affairs.

It was just before the "term." Mr.
Menteith had been expected all day, but
had not arrived; and the Earl had
taken a long drive with Helen and her
father through the Cairnforth woods, where
the wild daffodils were beginning to succeed the fading snowdrops, and the mavises
had been heard to sing those few rich
notes which belong especially to the twilights of early spring, an earnest of all

the richness and glory and delight of the year. The little party seemed to feel it — that soft, dreamy sense of dawning spring, which stirs all the soul, especially in youth, with a vague looking forward to some pleasantness which never comes. They sat, silent and talking by turns, beside the not unwelcome fire, in a corner of the large library.

"We shall miss Alick a good deal this spring," said Helen, recurring to a subject of which the family heart was full, the departure of the eldest son to begin the world in Mr. Menteith's office in Edinburgh. He was not a very clever lad, but he was sensible and steady; and blessed with that practical mother-wit which is often better than brains. The minister, though he had been bemoaning his boy's "little Latin and less Greek," and comparing Alick's learning very disadvantageously with that of the Earl — to whom Mr. Cardross confided all his troubles, nevertheless seemed both proud and hopeful of his eldest son — the heir to his honest name, which Alick would now carry out into a far wider world than that of the poor minister of Cairnforth, and doubtless in good time transmit honourably to a third generation.

"Yes," added the father — when innumerable castles in the air had been built and rebuilt for Alick's future — "I'll not deny that my lad is a good lad. He is the hope of the house, and he knows it.

It's little of worldly gear that he'll get for many a day, and he tells me he will have to work from morning till night — but he rather enjoys the prospect than not."

" No wonder. Work must be a happy thing," said, with a sigh, the young Earl of Cairnforth.

Helen's heart smote her for having let the conversation drift into this direction — as it did occasionally, when from their long familiarity with him, they forgot how he must feel about many things, natural enough to them, but to him, unto whom the outer world, with all its duties, energies, enjoyments, could never be any thing but a name — full of sharpest pain.

She said — after a few minutes watching of the grave, still face — not exactly sad, but only very still, very grave, —

"Just look at papa, how happy he is! among those books you sent for. Your plan of his arranging the library is the delight of his life."

"Is it? I am so glad," said the Earl, brightening up at once. "What a good thing I thought of it!"

"You always do think of every thing that is good and kind," said Helen, softly.

"Thank you," and the shadow passed away — as any trifling pleasure always had power to make it pass. Sometimes Helen speculated vaguely on what a grand sort of man the Earl would have been had he been like other people — how cheerful, how active, how energetic and wise! But then one never knows how far circumstances create and unfold character. We often learn as much by what is withheld as by what is enjoyed.

"Helen," he said, moving his chair a little nearer her — he had brought one good thing from London, a self-acting chair, in which he could wheel himself about easily, and liked doing it — "I wonder whether your father would have taken as much pleasure in his books thirty years ago. Do you think one could fill up one's whole life with reading and study?"

"I cannot say — I'm not clever myself, you know."

"Oh, but you are — with a sort of

practical cleverness. And so is Alick, in his own way. How happy Alick must be — going out into the world, with plenty to do all day long! How bright he looked this morning! "

" He sees only the sunny side of things: he is still no more than a boy."

" Not exactly — he is a year older than I am."

Helen hardly knew what to reply. She guessed so well the current of the Earl's thoughts — which were often her own too, as she watched his absent or weary looks, though he tried hard to keep his attention to what Mr. Cardross was reading or discussing. But the distance between twenty and sixty — the life beginning

and the life advancing towards its close —
was frequently apparent. Also, between
an active, original mind, requiring humanity
for its study, and one whose whole bent
was among the dry bones of ancient
learning. The difference, in short, between
learning and knowledge — the mere student
and the man who only uses study as a
means to the perfecting of his whole
nature, his complete existence as a human
being.

All this Helen felt with her quick,
feminine instinct, but she did not clearly
understand it, and she could not reason
about it at all. She only answered in a
troubled sort of way, that she thought
everybody, somehow or other, might in

time find enough to do — to be happy in doing — and she was trying to put her meaning into more connected and intelligible form, when, greatly to her relief, Malcolm entered the library.

Malcolm, being so necessary and close a personal attendant on the Earl, always came and went about his master without anybody's noticing him — but now Helen fancied he was making signals to her, or to some one. Lord Cairnforth detected them.

"Is any thing wrong, Malcolm? Speak out — don't hide things from me. I am not a child now."

There was just the slightest touch of sharpness in the gentle voice — and Malcolm did speak out.

"I wadna be troubling ye, my Lord:— but it's just an auld man, Dougal Mac Dougal, frae the head o' Loch Mhor—a puir, doited body, wha says he maun hae a bit word wi' your Lordship. But I tellt him ye couldna be fashed wi' the likes o' him."

"That was not civil or right, Malcolm. An old man, too. Where is he?"

"Just by the door—Eh—and he's coming ben—the ill-mannered loon!" cried Malcolm, angrily, as he interrupted the intruder—a tall, gaunt figure wrapt in a shepherd's plaid, with the bonnet set upon the grizzled head, in that sturdy inde- pendence—nay, more than independence— rudeness, rough and thorny as his own thistle, which is the characteristic of the

Scotch peasant externally, till you get below the surface to the warm, kindly heart.

"I'm no ill-mannered, and I'll just gang through the hale house till I find my Lord," said the old man, shaking off Malcolm with a strength that his seventy odd years seemed scarcely to have diminished. "I'm wushing nae harm to ony o' ye, but I maun get speech o' my Lord. He's no a bairn: he'll be ane-and-twenty the thirtieth o' June— I mind the day weel, for the wife was brought to bed o' her last wean the same day as the Countess, and our Dougal's a braw callant the noo, ye ken. Gin the Earl has ony wits ava, whilk folk thocht was aye doubtfu', he'll hae gotten

them by this time. I maun speak wi'
himsel'. Unless, as they said, he's no a'
there."

"Haud your tongue, ye fule!" cried
Malcolm, stopping him with a fierce
whisper. "Yon's my Lord!"

The old shepherd started back — for at
this moment a sudden blaze-up of the fire
showed, sitting in the corner, the dimi-
nutive figure; attired carefully after the
then fashion of gentlemen's dress; every
thing rich and complete — even to the
black silk stockings and shoes on the
small, useless feet, and the white ruffles
half hiding the twisted wrists and deformed hands.

"Yes — I am the Earl of Cairnforth.
What did you want to say to me?"

He was so bewildered — the rough shepherd, who had spent all his life on the hill-sides, and never seen or imagined so sad a sight as this, that at first he could not find a word. Then he said, hanging back and speaking confusedly and humbly, "I ask your pardon, my Lord — I didna ken — I'll no trouble ye the day."

"But you do not trouble me at all. Mr. Menteith is not here yet; and I know nothing about business — still if you wished to speak to me, do so: I am Lord Cairnforth."

"Are ye?" said the shepherd, evidently bewildered still, so that he forgot his natural awe for his feudal superior. "Are ye the Countess's bairn, that's just the age o' our Dougal? Dougal's ane o' the gamekeepers, ye ken — sic a braw fellow — sax feet three. — Ye'll hae seen him maybe?"

"No — but I should like to see him. And yourself; are you a tenant of mine, and what did you want with me?"

Encouraged by the kindly voice, and his own self-interest becoming prominent once more, old Dougal told his tale. Not an uncommon one — of sheep lost on the hill-side, and one misfortune following another, until a large family, children and orphan grandchildren, were driven at last to want the "sup o' parritch" for daily food — sinking to such depths of poverty as the Earl in his secluded life had never even heard of. And yet the proud old fellow asked nothing, except the remission of one year's rent, after having paid rent honestly for half a lifetime. That stolid, silent endurance, which makes a Scotch beggar, of any sort, about the last thing you ever meet with in Scotland, supported him to the very end.

The Earl was deeply touched. As a matter of course he promised all that was desired of him, and sent the old shepherd away happy; but long after Dougal's departure. he sat thoughtful and grave.

"Can such things be, Helen, and I never heard of them? Are some of my people — they are my people, since the land belongs to me — as terribly poor as that man?"

"Ay, very many, though papa looks after them as much as he can. Dougal is out of his parish — or he would have known him. Papa knows every body, and takes care of every body, as far as possible."

" So ought I — or I must do it when I am older," said the Earl, thoughtfully.

" There will be no difficulty about that when you come of age and enter on your property."

" Is it a very large property ? for I never heard or inquired."

" Very large."

" Show me its boundary — there is the map."

Helen took it down and drew with a pencil the limits of the Cairnforth estates. They extended along the whole peninsula, and far up into the mainland.

" There, Lord Cairnforth. Every bit of this is yours."

" To do exactly what I like with ? "

" Certainly."

" Helen, it is an awfully serious thing."

Helen was silent.

" How strange!" he continued, after a pause. " And this was really all mine, from the very hour of my birth ? "

" Yes."

" And when I come of age I shall have to take my property into my own hands and manage it just as I choose, or as I can ? "

" Of course you will. And I think you can do it — if you try."

For it was not the first time that

Helen had pondered over these things: since, being neither learned nor poetical, worldly-minded nor selfish, in her silent hours her mind generally wandered to the practical concerns of other people, and especially of those she loved.

"' Try' ought to be the motto of the Cardross arms — of yours certainly," said Lord Cairnforth, smiling. "I should like to assume it on mine — instead of my own 'Virtute et fide,' which is of little use to me. How can I — *I* — be brave or faithful?"

. "You can be both — and you will," said Helen, softly. Years from that day she remembered what she had said — and how true it was.

A little while afterwards, while the

minister still remained buried in his be-loved books, Lord Cairnforth recurred again to Dougal MacDougal.

" The old fellow was right. If I am ever to have ' ony wits ava,' I ought to have them by this time. I am nearly twenty-one. Any other young man would have been a man long ago. And I will be a man — why should I not? True manliness is not solely outside. I daresay you could find many a fool and a coward six feet high."

" Yes," answered Helen, all she could find to say.

" And if I have nothing else, I have brains — quite as good brains, I think, as my neighbours. They cannot say of me now that I'm ' no a' there.' Nay,

Helen, don't look so · fierce, they meant me no ill — it was but natural. Yes, God has left me something to be thankful for."

The Earl lifted his head — the only part of his· whole frame which he could move freely ; and his eyes flashed under his broad brows. Thoroughly manly brows they were, wherein any acute observer might trace that clear, sound sense, active energy, and indomitable persever- ance which make the real man — and lacking which, the "brawest" young fellow alive is a mere body — an animal wanting the soul.

" I wonder how I should set about managing my property. The duty will not be as easy for me as for most people, you know," added he, sadly. "Still, if I had a secretary, — a thorough man of business, to teach me all about business, and to be constantly at my side, perhaps I might be able to accomplish it. And I might drive about the country — driving is less painful to me now — and get acquainted with my people; see what they wanted, and how I could best help them. They would get used to me, too. I might turn out to be a very respectable laird, and become interested in the improvement of my estates."

"There is great opportunity for that, I know," replied Helen. And then she told him of a conversation she had heard between her father and Mr. Menteith : when the latter had spoken of great changes impending over quiet Cairnforth : how a steamer was to begin plying up and down the loch — how there were continual applications for land to be feued — and how all these improvements would of necessity require the owner of the soil to take many a step unknown to and undreamed of by his forefathers — to make roads, reclaim hill and moorland, build new farms, churches, and school-houses.

" In short, as Mr. Menteith said, the world is changing so fast that the present Earl of Cairnforth will have anything but the easy life of his father and grandfather."

" Did Mr. Menteith say that ? " cried the Earl, eagerly.

" He did, indeed — I heard him."

" And did he seem to think that I should be able for it ? "

" I cannot tell," answered truthful Helen. " He said not a word one way or the other, about your being capable of doing the work : he only said the work was to be done."

" Then I will try and do it."

The Earl said this quietly enough — but his eyes gleamed and his lips quivered.

Helen laid her hand upon his — much moved. " I said you were brave — always. Still, you must think twice about it ; for it will be a very responsible duty. Enough, Mr. Menteith told papa, to require a

 A Noble Life.

man's whole energies for the next twenty years."

" I wonder if I shall live so long. Well, I am glad, Helen. It will be something worth living for."

Chapter the Seventh.

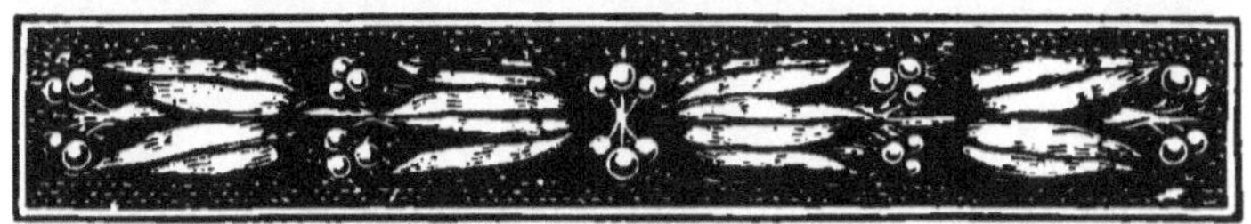

MALCOLM'S saying, that "if my Lord taks a thing into his head he'll aye do't, ye ken," was as true now as when the Earl was a little boy.

Mr. Menteith hardly knew how the thing was accomplished, indeed he had rather opposed it, believing the mere physical impediments to his ward's overlooking his own affairs were insurmountable: but Lord Cairnforth contrived in the course of a day or two to initiate himself very fairly in all the business attendant upon the "term:" to find out the exact extent and divisions of his property, and to whom it was feued. And on term-day he proposed, though with an evident effort which touched the old lawyer deeply, — to sit beside Mr. Menteith while the tenants were paying their rents, so as to become personally known to each of them.

Many of these, like Dougal Mac Dougal, were overcome with surprise, — nay, something more painful than surprise, at sight of the small figure which was the last descendant of the noble Earls of Cairnforth, and with whom the stalwart father and the fair young mother, looking down from the pictured walls, contrasted so piteously; but after the first shock was over, they carried away only the remembrance of his sweet, grave face, and his intelligent and pertinent observations, indicating a shrewdness for which even Mr. Menteith was unprepared. When he owned this — after business was done — the young Earl smiled, evidently much gratified.

"Yes; I don't think they can say of me that I'm 'no a' there!'" Also he, that evening, confessed to Helen that he found "business" nearly as interesting as Greek and Latin, perhaps even more so, for there was something human in it, something which drew one closer to one's fellow-creatures, and benefited other people besides oneself. "I think," he added, "I should rather enjoy being what is called 'a good man of business.'"

He pleaded so hard for further instruction in all pertaining to his estate that Mr. Menteith consented to spare two whole weeks out of his busy Edinburgh life, during which Lord Cairnforth and he were shut up together for a great part of every day, investigating matters connected with the property, and other things in which hitherto the young man's education had been entirely neglected.

"For," said his guardian, sadly, "I own I never thought of him as a young man — or as a man at all: nevertheless, he is one, and will always be. That clear, cool head of his, just for brains, pure brains, is worth both his father's and grandfather's put together."

And when Helen repeated this saying to

Lord Cairnforth, he smiled his exceedingly bright smile, and was more than cheerful, joyous, for days after.

On Mr. Menteith's return home, he sent back to the Castle one of his old clerks, who had been acquainted with the Cairnforth affairs for nearly half-a-century: he also was astonished at the capacity which the young Earl showed. Of course, physically, he was entirely helpless: the little forked stick was still in continual requsition: nor could he write except with much difficulty. But he had the faculty of arrangement and order, and the rare power, rarer than is supposed, of guiding and governing; so that what he could not do himself he could direct others how to do, and thus attain his end so perfectly, that even those who knew him best were oftentimes actually amazed at the result he effected.

Then he enjoyed his work: took such an interest in the plans for feuing land along the loch-side: and the sort of houses that were to be built upon each feu: the roads he would have to make, and especially the grand wooden pier, which, by Mr. Menteith's advice, was shortly to be erected in lieu of the little quay of stones at the ferry, which had hitherto served as Cairnforth's chief link with the outside world.

If Mr. Cardross and Helen grieved a little over this advancing tide of civilisation, which might soon sweep away many things old and dear from the shores of beautiful Loch Beg, they grew reconciled when they saw the light in the Earl's eyes, and heard him talk with an interest and enthusiasm quite new to him, of what he meant to do when he came of age. Only in all his projects was one peculiarity, rather uncommon in young heirs: the entire absence of any schemes for personal pleasure. Comforts he had, of course: his faithful friends and servants took care that his condition should have every alleviation that wealth could furnish. But of enjoyments, after the fashion of youth, he planned nothing; for indeed what of them was left him to enjoy?

And so, faster than usual — being so well filled with occupations — the weeks and months slipped by, until the important thirtieth of June; when Mr. Menteith's term of guardianship would end; and a man's free life and independent duties, so far as he could perform them, would legally begin for the Earl of Cairnforth.

There had been great consultations on this topic all along the two lochs — and beyond them: for Dougal MacDougal had carried his story of the Earl and his goodness to the extreme verge of the Cairnforth territory. Throughout June the Manse was weekly haunted by tenants, arriving from all quarters, to consult the minister, the universal referee, as to how they could best celebrate the event, which, whenever it occurred, had for generations been kept gloriously in the little peninsula — though no case was known of any

Earl's attaining his majority as being already Earl of Cairnforth. The Montgomeries were usually a long-lived race — and their heirs rarely came to their titles till middle-aged fathers of families.

"But we maun hae grand doings this time, ye ken," said an old farmer to the minister, "for I doubt there 'll ne'er be anither Earl o' Cairnforth."

Which fact every one seemed sorrowfully to recognise. It was not only probable, but right, that in this Lord Cairnforth, — so terribly afflicted — the long line should end.

As the day of the Earl's majority approached, the minister's feelings were of such a mingled kind that he shrank from these demonstrations of joy, and rather repressed the warm loyalty which was springing up everywhere towards the young man. But after taking counsel with Helen, who saw into things a little deeper than he did, Mr. Cardross decided that it was better all should be done exactly as if the present lord were not different from his forefathers, and that he should be helped both to act and to feel as like other people as possible.

Therefore, on a bright June morning, as bright as that of his sad birth-day and his mother's death-day, twenty-one years before, the Earl awoke to the sound of music playing — if the national pipes of the peninsula could be called music — underneath his window; and heard his good neighbours from the clachan, young and old, men, women, and bairns, uniting their voices in one hearty shout, wishing "A lang life and a merry ane" to the Earl of Cairnforth.

Whether or not the young man's heart echoed the wish, who could tell? It was among the solemn secrets which every human soul has to keep, and ever must keep, — between itself and its Maker.

Very soon the Earl appeared out-of-doors, wheeling himself along the terrace in his little chair; answering smilingly the congratulations of everybody, and evidently enjoying the pleasant morning, the sunshine, and the scent of the flowers in what was still called "the Countess's garden." People noticed afterwards how very like he looked that day to his beautiful mother; and many a mother out of the clachan, who remembered the lady's face still, and how, during her few brief months of married happiness and hope, she used to stop her pretty pony-carriage to notice every poor woman's baby she chanced to pass, — many of these now regarded pitifully and tenderly her only son — the last heir of the last Countess of Cairnforth.

Yet he certainly enjoyed himself: there could be no doubt of it; and when, later in the day, he discovered a conspiracy between the Castle, the Manse, and the clachan, which resulted in a grand feast on the lawn, he was highly delighted.

"All this for me!" he cried, almost childish in his pleasure. "How good everybody is to me!"

And he insisted on mixing with the little crowd, and seeing them sit down to their banquet: which they ate as if they had never eaten in their lives before, and drank — as Highlanders can drink ; and Highlanders alone. But before the whisky began to grow dangerous, the oldest man among the tenantry, who declared that he could remember three Earls of Cairnforth, proposed the health of this Earl, which was received with acclamations long and loud—the pipers playing the family tune of "Montgomerie's Reel,"—which was chiefly notable for having neither beginning, middle, nor ending.

Lord Cairnforth bowed his head in acknowledgment.

"Ought not somebody to make a little

speech of thanks to them?" whispered he to Helen Cardross, who stood close behind his chair.

"You should; and I think you could," was her answer.

"Very well.   I will try."

And in his poor feeble voice, which trembled much, yet was distinct and clear, he said a few words, very short and simple, to the people near him.   He thanked them for all this merry-making in his honour, and said "he was exceedingly happy that day."   He told them he meant always to reside at Cairnforth, and to carry out all sorts of plans for the improvement of his estates, both for his tenants' benefit and his own.   That he hoped to be both a just and kind landlord, working with and for his tenantry to the utmost of his power.

"That is," he added, with a slight fall of the voice, "to the utmost of those few powers which it has pleased Heaven to give me."

After this speech there was a full minute's silence,—tender, touching silence, and then arose a cheer, long and loud, such as had rarely echoed through the little peninsula on the coming of age of any Lord Cairnforth.

When the tenantry had gone away to light bonfires on the hill-side, and perform many other feats of jubilation, a little dinner-party assembled in the large dining-room, which had been so long disused, for the Earl always preferred the library,

which was on a level with his bed-room,
whence he could wheel himself in and
out as he pleased. To-day, the family
table was outspread, and the family plate
glittered; and the family portraits stared
down from the wall as the last Earl of
Cairnforth moved — or rather was moved —
slowly down the long room. Malcolm was
wheeling him to a side seat well sheltered
and comfortable, when he said, —

"Stop! — Remember I am twenty-one
to-day. I think I ought to take my seat
at the head of my own table."

Malcolm obeyed. And thus, for the
first time since the late Earl's death, the
place — the master's place — was filled.

"Mr. Cardross, will you say grace?"

The minister tried once — twice — thrice;

but his voice failed him. His tender heart, which had lived through so many losses, and this day saw all the past brought before him, vivid as yesterday, entirely broke down. Thereupon the Earl, from his seat at the head of his own table, repeated simply and naturally the few words, which every head of a household —as priest in his own family — may well say.

"For these and all other mercies, Lord, make us thankful."

After that, Mr. Menteith took snuff vehemently, and Mr. Cardross openly wiped his eyes. But Helen's, if not quite dry, were very bright. Her woman's heart, which looked beyond the pain of suffering into the beauty of suffering nobly endured, even as faith looks through "the grave and gate of death" into the glories of immortality — Helen's heart was scarcely sad, but very glad and proud.

The day after Lord Cairnforth's coming of age, Mr. Menteith formally resigned his trust. He had managed the property so successfully during the long minority, that even he himself was surprised at the amount of money, both capital and income, which the Earl was now master of, without restriction or reservation, and free from the control of any human being.

"Yes, my Lord," said he, when the young man seemed subdued and almost overcome by the extent of his own wealth, "it is really all your own. You may make ducks and drakes of it, as the saying goes, as soon as ever you please. You are accountable for it to no one — except One," added the good, honest, religious man — now growing an old man, and a little gentler, graver, as well as a little more demonstrative than he had been twenty years before.

" Except One. I know that: I hope I shall never forget it," replied the Earl of Cairnforth.

And then they proceeded to wind up their business affairs.

" How strange it is," observed the Earl, when they had nearly concluded —" how very strange that I should be here in the world, an isolated human being, with not a single blood relation, not a soul who has any real claim upon me."

"Certainly not: no claim whatsoever: and yet you are not quite without blood relations."

Lord Cairnforth looked surprised. "I always understood that I had no near kindred."

"Of near kindred you have none. But there are certain far-away cousins: of whom, for many reasons, I never told you — and begged Mr. Cardross not to tell you either."

"I think — I ought to have been told."

Mr. Menteith explained his strong reasons for silence: such as the late Lord's unpleasant experience — and his own — of the Bruce family: and the necessity he saw for keeping his ward quite out of their association and their influence till his character was matured, and he was of an age to judge for himself, and act for himself, concerning them. All the more, because, remote as their kinship was, and difficult to be proved, still, if proved, they would be undoubtedly his next heirs.

" My next heirs," repeated the Earl — " of course: I must have an heir. I wonder I never thought of that. If I died, there must be somebody to succeed me in the title and estates."

" Not in the title," said Mr. Menteith, hesitating — for he saw it was opening a subject most difficult and painful, yet which must be opened some time or other; and the old man was too honest to shrink from so doing, if necessary.

"Why not the title?"

"It is entailed: and can be inherited in the direct male line only."

"That is, it descends from father to son?"

"Exactly so."

"I see," said the young man, after a long pause. "Then, I am the last Earl of Cairnforth."

There was no answer. Mr. Menteith could not for his life have given one. Besides none seemed required. The Earl said it as if merely stating a fact, beyond which there is no appeal — and neither expecting nor desiring any refutation or contradiction.

" Now," Lord Cairnforth continued, suddenly changing the conversation —" let us speak once more of the Bruces, who, you say, might any day succeed to my fortune, and would probably make a very bad use of it."

" I believe so: upon my conscience I do ! " said Mr. Menteith, earnestly — " else I never should have felt justified in keeping them out of your way as I have done."

" Who are they ? I mean of what does the family consist ? "

" An old man — Colonel Bruce he calls himself: and is known as such in every disreputable gambling town on the Continent : a long tribe of girls, and one son, eldest or youngest, I forget which, who was sent to India, through some influence I used for your father's sake;—but who may be dead by now for aught I know. Indeed, the utmost I have had to do with the family of late years has been paying the annuity granted them by the late Earl; which I continued, not legally, but through charity—on trust that the present Earl would never call me to account for the same."

"Most certainly I never shall."

"Then you will take my advice—and forgive my intruding upon you a little more of it?"

"Forgive? I am thankful, my good old friend, for every wise word you say to me."

Again the good lawyer hesitated.

"There is a subject, one exceedingly difficult to speak of—but it should be named; since you might not think of it yourself. Lord Cairnforth, the only way in which you can secure your property against these Bruces is by at once making your will."

"Making my will!" replied the Earl, looking as if the new · responsibilities opening upon him were almost bewildering.

"Every man who has anything to leave ought to make a will as soon as ever he comes of age. Vainly I urged this upon your father."

"My poor father! That he should die — so young and strong — and I should live — how strange it seems! You think, then — perhaps Dr. Hamilton also thinks — that my life is precarious?"

“ I cannot tell ; my dear Lord, how could any man possibly tell ?”

“ Well — it will not make me die one day sooner or later to have made my will’: as you say, every man ought to do it ; I ought especially, for my life is more doubtful than most people’s. And it is a solemn charge to possess so large a fortune as mine.”

“ Yes. The good — or harm — that might be done with it, is incalculable.”

“ I feel that : at least I am beginning to feel it.”

And for a time the Earl sat silent and thoughtful : the old lawyer fussing about — putting papers and *débris* of all sorts into their right places, but feeling it awkward to resume the conversation.

"Mr. Menteith, are you at liberty now? For I have quite made up my mind. This matter of the will shall be settled at once. It can be done?"

"Certainly."

"Sit down then, and I will dictate it. But first you must promise not to interfere with any disposition I may see fit to make of my property."

"I should not have the slightest right to do so, Lord Cairnforth."

"My good old friend! — Well, now, how shall we begin?"

"I should recommend your first stating any legacies you may wish to leave: — to dependents—for instance, Mrs. Campbell, or Malcolm — and then bequeathing the whole bulk of your estates to some one person,—

some young person, likely to outlive you, and upon whom you can depend to carry out all your plans and intentions, and make as good a use of your fortune as you would have done yourself. That is my principle as to choice of an heir. There are many instances in which blood is *not* thicker than water — and a friend, by election, is often worthier and dearer — besides being closer — than any relative."

"You are right."

"Still, consanguinity must be considered a little. You might leave a certain sum to these Bruces — or, if on inquiry you found among them any child whom you approved, you could adopt him as your heir, and he could take the name of Montgomerie."

" No," replied the Earl, decisively. " That name is ended. All I have to consider is my own people here—my tenants and servants. Whoever succeeds me ought to know them all, and be to them exactly what I have been — or rather what I hope to be."

" Mr. Cardross, for instance. Were you thinking of him as your heir?"

" No, not exactly," replied Lord Cairn-forth, slightly colouring. " He is a little too old. Besides, he is not quite the sort of person I should wish : too gentle and self-absorbed — too little practical."

" One of his sons, perhaps?"

" No — nor one of yours either ; to whom, by the way, you will please to set down a thousand pounds a-piece. Nay,

don't look so horrified — it will not harm
them.   But personally I do not know
them, nor they me.   And my heir
should be some one whom I thoroughly
do know, thoroughly respect, thoroughly
love.   There is but one person in the
world — one young person — who answers
to all these requisites."

"Who is that?"

"Helen Cardross."

Mr. Menteith was a good deal surprised.   Though he had a warm corner
in his heart for Helen — still, the idea
of her as heiress to so large an estate
was novel and startling.   He did not
consider himself justified in criticising the
Earl's choice — still, he thought it odd.
True, Helen was a brave, sensible, self-

dependent woman; not a girl any longer;
— and accustomed from the age of fifteen to
guide a household, to be her father's right
hand, and her brothers' help and coun-
sellor — one of those rare characters who,
without being exactly masculine, are yet
not too feebly feminine — in whom strength
is never exaggerated to boldness, nor gentleness deteriorated into weakness. She was
firm, too; could form her own opinion and
carry it out; though not accomplished, was
fairly well educated; possessed plenty of
sound practical knowledge of men and
things, and above all, had habits of extreme order and regularity. People said,
sometimes, that Miss Cardross ruled not
only the Manse, but the whole parish;
however, if so, she did it in so sweet a

way that nobody ever objected to her government.

All these things Mr. Menteith ran over in his acute mind within the next few minutes, during which he did not commit himself to any remarks at all. At last he said,—

" I think, my Lord, you are right. Helen's no bonnie; but she is a rare creature; with the head of a man and the heart of a woman. She is worth all her brothers put together, and under the circumstances, I believe you could not do better than make her your heiress."

" I am glad you think so," was the brief answer. Though, by the expression of the Earl's face, Mr. Menteith clearly saw that, whether he had thought it or not, the result would have been just the same. He smiled a little to himself; but he did not dispute the matter. He knew that one of the best qualities the Earl possessed, most blessed and useful to him — as it is to every human being — was the power of making up his own mind, and acting upon it with that quiet resolution which is quite distinct from obstinacy, — obstinacy, usually the last stronghold of cowards, and the blustering self-defence of fools.

"There is but one objection to your plan, Lord Cairnforth. Miss Cardross is young — twenty-six, I think."

"Twenty-five and a half."

"She may not remain always Miss Card-ross. She may marry; and we cannot tell what sort of man her husband may be, or how fit to be trusted with so large a property."

"So good a woman is not likely to choose a man unworthy of her," said Lord Cairnforth, after a pause. "Still, could not my fortune be settled upon herself as a life-rent, to descend intact to her heirs, that is, her children?"

"My dear Lord! how you must have thought over every thing!"

"You forget, my friend — I have nothing to do but to sit thinking."

There was a sad intonation in the voice, which affected Mr. Menteith deeply. He made no remark, but busied himself in drawing up the will, which Lord Cairnforth seemed nervously anxious should be completed that very day.

"For, suppose anything should happen; if I died this night, for instance! No, let what is done be done as soon as possible, and as privately."

"You wish, then, the matter to be kept private?" asked Mr. Menteith.

"Yes."

So in the course of the next few hours the will was drawn up. It was somewhat voluminous with sundry small legacies; no one being forgotten whom the Earl desired to benefit or thought needed his help; but the bulk of his fortune he left unreservedly to Helen Cardross. Malcolm and another servant were called in as witnesses — and the Earl, saying to them with a cheerful smile "that he was making his will, but did not mean to die a day the sooner," signed it with that feeble, uncertain signature which yet had cost him years of pains to acquire, and never might have been acquired at all, but for his own perseverance and the unwearied patience of Helen Cardross.

"She taught me to write, you know," said he to Mr. Menteith, as — the witnesses being gone — he, with a half-amused look, regarded his own autograph.

"You have used the results of her teaching well on her behalf to-day. It is no trifle—a clear income of ten thousand a-year: but she will make a good use of it."

"I am sure of that. So now, all is safe and right: and I may die as soon as God pleases."

He leaned his head back wearily; and his face was overspread by that melancholy shadow which it wore at times; showing how, at best, life was a heavy burthen — as it could not but be — to him.

"Come now," said the Earl, rousing himself, "we have still a good many things to talk over, which I want to consult you about before you go."

Whereupon the young man opened up such a number of schemes, chiefly for the benefit of his tenantry and the neighbourhood, that Mr. Menteith was quite overwhelmed.

"Why, my Lord, you are the most energetic Earl of Cairnforth that ever came to the title. It would take three lifetimes, instead of a single one, even if that reached threescore and ten, to carry out all you want to do."

"Would it? Then let us hope it was not for nothing that those good folk yesterday made themselves hoarse with wishing me 'a lang life and a merry ane.' And when I die —— but we'll not enter upon that subject. My dear old friend, I hope for many and many a thirtieth of June I shall make you welcome to Cairnforth. And now let us take a quiet drive together, and fetch all the Manse people up to dinner at the Castle."

Chapter the Eighth.

THE same evening, the Earl and his guests were sitting in the June twilight — the long, late northern twilight, which is nowhere more lovely than on the shores of Loch Beg. Malcolm had just come in with candles, as a gentle hint that it was time for his master — over whose personal welfare he was sometimes a little too solicitous — to retire, when there happened what for the time being, startled everybody present.

Malcolm, going to the window, sprang suddenly back with a shout and a scream.

"I kent it weel. It was sure to be! Oh, my Lord, my Lord!"

"What is the matter?" said Mr. Menteith sharply. "You're gone daft, man;" for the big Highlander was trembling like a child.

"Whisht! dinna speak o't. It was my Lord's wraith, ye ken. It just keekit in and slippit awa."

"Folly! I saw nothing."

"But I think I did," said Lord Cairn-forth.

"Hear him! — Ay, he saw 't, his ain sel. Then it maun be true. Oh, my dear Lord!"

Poor Malcolm fell on his knees by the Earl's little chair in such agitation that Mr. Cardross looked up from his book, and

Helen from her peaceful needle-work, which was rarely out of her active hands.

"He thinks he has seen his master's wraith; and because the Earl signed his will this morning, he is sure to die — especially as Lord Cairnforth saw the same thing himself. Will you say, my Lord, what you did see?"

"Mr. Menteith, I believe I saw a man peering in at that window."

"It wasna a man — it was a speerit," moaned Malcolm. "My Lord's wraith, for sure."

"I don't think so, Malcolm. For it was a tall thin figure that moved about lightly and airily — was come and gone in a moment. Not very like my wraith — unless the wraith of myself as what I might have been."

The little party were silent: till Helen said,—

"What do you think it was then?"

"Certainly a man ; made of honest flesh and blood — though not much of either, for he was excessively thin and sickly-looking.　He just 'keekit in,' as Malcolm says, and disappeared."

"What a very odd circumstance!" said Mr. Menteith.　"Not a robber, I trust. I am much more afraid of robbers than of ghosts."

"We never rob at Cairnforth: we are very honest people here.　No; I think it is far likelier to be one of these stray tourists who are brought here by the steamers.　They sometimes take great liberties, wandering into the Castle grounds, and, perhaps, one of them thought he might as well come and stare in at my windows."

"I hope he was English: I should not like a Scotsman to do such a rude thing," cried Helen indignantly.

Lord Cairnforth laughed at her impulsiveness. There was much of the child nature mingled in Helen's gravity and wisdom; and she sometimes did both speak and act from impulse — especially generous and kindly impulse — as hastily and unthinkingly as a child.

"Well, Malcolm, the only way to settle this difficulty is to search the house and grounds. Take a good thick stick and a lantern: and whatever you find — be it tourist or burglar, man or spirit — bring him at once to me."

And then the little group waited — laughing among themselves; but still not quite at ease. Lord Cairnforth would not allow Mr. Cardross and Helen to walk home; the carriage was ordered to be made ready.

Presently Malcolm appeared — somewhat crestfallen.

"It is a man, my Lord; and no speerit. But he wadna come ben. He says he 'll wait your lordship's will; and that's his name," laying a card before the Earl, who looked at it and started with surprise.

"Mr. Menteith, just see — 'Captain Ernest Henry Bruce.' What an odd coincidence!"

"Coincidence indeed!" repeated the lawyer, sceptically. "Let me see the card."

"Ernest Henry! was that the name of the young man whom you sent out to India?"

"How should I remember? It was ten or fifteen years ago. Very annoying! However, since he is a Bruce — or says he is — I suppose your lordship must just see him."

"Certainly," replied, in his quiet, determined tone, the Earl of Cairnforth.

Helen, who looked exceedingly surprised, offered to retire; but the Earl would not hear of it.

"No, no; you are a wise woman, and an acute one, too. I would like you to see and judge of this cousin of mine — a far-away cousin, who would like well enough, Mr. Menteith guesses, to be my heir. But we will not judge him harshly, and especially we will not prejudge him. His father was nothing to boast of, but this may be a very honest man for all we know. Sit by me, Helen, and take a good look at him."

And with a certain amused pleasure the Earl watched Helen's puzzled air at being made of so much importance, till the stranger appeared.

He was a man of about thirty; though at first sight he seemed older, from his exceedingly worn and sickly appearance. His lank black hair fell about his thin, sallow face; he wore what we now call the Byron collar and Byron tie — for it was in the Byron era, when sentimentalism and misery-making were all the fashion.

Certainly the poor Captain looked miserable enough, without any pretence of it; for besides his thin and unhealthy aspect, his attire was in the lowest depth of genteel shabbiness. Nevertheless, he looked gentlemanly, and clever too; nor was it an unpleasant face, though the lower half of it indicated weakness and indecision; and the eyes — large, dark, and hollow — were a little too closely set together, a peculiarity which always gives an uncandid, and often a rather sinister expression to any face. Still, there was something about the unexpected visitor decidedly interesting.

Even Helen looked up from her work — once — twice — with no small curiosity; she saw so few strangers; and of men, and young men, almost none, from year's end to year's end. Yet it was a look as frank, as unconscious, as maidenly, as might have been Miranda's first glance at Ferdinand.

Captain Bruce did not return her glance at all. His whole attention was engrossed by Lord Cairnforth.

"My Lord, I am so sorry — so very sorry — if I startled you by my rudeness. The group inside was so cheering a sight; and I was a poor, weary wayfarer."

"Do not apologise, Captain Bruce. I am happy to make your acquaintance."

"It has been the wish of my life, Lord Cairnforth, to make yours."

Lord Cairnforth turned upon him eyes sharp enough to make a less acute person than the Captain feel that honesty, rather than flattery, was the safest tack to go upon. He took the hint.

"That is, I have wished, ever since I came home from India, to thank you, and Mr. Menteith — this is Mr. Menteith, I presume ? — for my cadetship which I got through you. And though my ill health has blighted my prospects, and after some service — for I exchanged from the Company's civil into the military service, — I have returned to England an invalided and disappointed man ; still my gratitude is exactly the same; and I was anxious to see and thank you, as my benefactor and my cousin."

Lord Cairnforth merely bent his head in answer to this long speech, which a little perplexed him.   He, like Helen, was both unused and indifferent to strangers.

But Captain Bruce seemed determined not to be made a stranger.   After the brief ceremony of introduction to the little party, he sat down close to Lord Cairnforth — displacing Helen, who quietly retired — and began to unfold all his circumstances, giving as credentials of identity a medal received for some Indian battle; a letter from his father, the Colonel, whose handwriting Mr. Menteith immediately recognised, and other data, which snfficiently proved that he really was the person he assumed to be.

"For," said he, with that exceedingly frank manner he had, the sort of manner particularly taking with reserved people, because it saves them so much trouble. "For otherwise how should you know that I am not an impostor — a swindler — instead of your cousin, which I hope you believe I really am, Lord Cairn-forth ?"

" Certainly," said the Earl, smiling, and looking both amused and interested by this little adventure — so novel in his monotonous life.

Also, his kindly heart was touched by the sickly and feeble aspect of the young man, by his appearance of poverty, and by something in his air which the Earl fancied implied that brave struggle against misfortune, more pathetic than misfortune itself. With undisguised pleasure, the young host sat and watched his guest doing full justice to the very best supper the Castle could furnish.

"You are truly a good Samaritan," said Captain Bruce, pouring out freely the claret which was then the universal drink of even the middle classes in Scotland. "I had fallen among thieves (literally, for my small baggage was stolen from me yesterday — and I have no worldly goods beyond the clothes I stand in); you meet me, my good cousin, with oil and wine, and set me on your own beast, which I fear I shall have to ask you to do, for I am not strong enough to walk any distance. How far is it to the nearest inn?"

"About twenty miles. But we will

discuss that question presently. In the meantime eat and drink. You need it."

" Ah, yes! You have never known hunger — I hope you never may; but it is not a pleasant thing, I assure you, actually to want food."

Helen looked up sympathetically. As Captain Bruce took not the slightest notice of her, she had ample opportunity to observe him. Pity for his worn face made her lenient: Lord Cairnforth read her favourable judgment in her eyes, and it inclined him also to judge kindly of the stranger. Mr. Menteith alone, more familiar with the wickedness of the world, and goaded by it into that sharp suspiciousness which is the last hardening of a kindly and generous heart — Mr. Menteith held aloof for some time; till at last even he succumbed to the charm of the Captain's conversation. Mr. Cardross had already fallen a willing victim; for he had latterly been deep in the subject of Warren Hastings, and to meet with any one who came direct from that wondrous land of India, then as mysterious and far-away a region as the next world — to people in England, and especially in the wilds of Scotland, was to the good minister a delight indescribable.

Captain Bruce, who had at first paid little attention to anybody but his cousin, soon exercised his faculty of being "all things to all men;" gave out his stores of information, bent all his varied powers to gratify Lord Cairnforth's friends, and succeeded.

The clock had struck twelve — and still the little party were gathered round the supper-table. Captain Bruce rose.

"I am ashamed to have detained you from your natural rest, Lord Cairnforth: I am but a poor sleeper myself: my cough often disturbs me much. Perhaps as there is no inn, one of your servants could direct me to some cottage near, where I could get a night's lodging and go on my way to-morrow. Any humble place will do: I am accustomed to rough it: besides it suits my finances — half-pay to a sickly invalid is hard enough — you understand?"

"I do."

"Still, if I could only get health! I have been told that this part of the country is very favourable to people with delicate lungs. Perhaps I might meet with some farm-house lodging?"

"I could not possibly allow that," said Lord Cairnforth, unable, in spite of all Mr. Menteith's grave, warning looks, to shut up his warm heart any longer. "The Castle is your home, Captain Bruce, for as long as you may find it pleasant to remain here."

The invitation, given so unexpectedly and cordially, seemed to surprise, nay, to touch the young man, extremely.

"Thank you, my cousin. You are very kind to me, which is more than I can say of the world in general. I will thankfully stay with you for a little. It might give me a chance of health."

" I trust so."

" Still, to make all clear between host and guest, let me name some end to my visit. This is the first day of July — may I accept your hospitality for a fortnight, — say till the 15th ? "

" Till whenever you please," replied the Earl, courteously and warmly. For he was pleased to find his cousin, even though a Bruce, so very agreeable : glad, too, that he had it in his power to do him a kindness which, perhaps, had too long been neglected. Besides, Lord Cairnforth had few friends, and youth so longs for companionship. This was actually the first time he had had a chance of forming an intimacy with a young man of his own age, education, and position ; and he caught at it with avidity. The more so, because Captain Bruce seemed likely to supply all the things which he had not, and never could have: knowledge of the world outside: " hair-breadth 'scapes " and adventurous experiences, told with a point and cleverness that added to their charm.

Besides, the Captain was decidedly " interesting." Young ladies would have thought him so, with his pale face and pensive air, which, seeing that the Byron fever had not yet attacked the youths of Cairnforth, appeared to his simple audience a melancholy quite natural, and not assumed. And his delicacy of health was a fact only too patent. There was a hectic brilliant colour on his cheek, and his cough interrupted him continually. His whole appearance implied that, in any case, a long life was scarcely probable; and this alone was enough to soften any tender heart towards him.

"What does Helen think of my new cousin?" whispered Lord Cairnforth, looking up to her with his affectionate eyes, as she bent over his chair to bid him good night.

"I like him," was the frank answer. "He is very agreeable, and then he looks so ill."

"Was I right in asking him to stay here?"

"Yes, I think so. He is your nearest relation, and, as the proverb says, 'Bluid is thicker than water.'"

"Not always."

"But now, you will soon be able to judge how you like him, and if you do like him, I hope you will be very kind to him."

"Do you, Helen? Then I certainly will."

The Earl kept his word. Many weeks went by; the 15th July was long past, and still Captain Bruce remained a guest at the Castle: quite domesticated; for he soon made himself as much at home as if he had dwelt there all his days. He fluctuated a little between the Castle and the Manse, but soon decided that the latter was "rather a dull house"—the boys rough, —the minister too much of a student— and Miss Cardross—"a very good sort of girl, but certainly no beauty." Which dictum, delivered in an oracular manner, as from one well accustomed to criticise the sex, always amused the Earl exceedingly.

To Lord Cairnforth, his new - found cousin devoted himself in the most cousinly way. Tender, respectful, unobtrusive — bestowing on him enough, and not too much, of his society; never interfering, and yet always at hand with any assistance required: he was exactly the companion which the Earl needed—and liked constantly beside him. For, of course, Malcolm, fond and faithful as he was, was only a servant. A friend, who was also a gentleman, yet who did not seem to feel or dislike the many small cares and attentions which were necessities to Lord Cairnforth, was quite a different thing. It was a touching contrast to see the two together; the active, elegant young man—for now he was well dressed, Captain Bruce looked remarkably elegant and gentlemanly; and the little motionless figure; as impassive and helpless almost as an image carved in stone, but yet who was undoubtedly the Earl of Cairnforth, and sole master of Cairnforth Castle.

Perhaps the wisest hit of the Captain's proceedings was the tact with which he always recognised this fact, and paid his cousin that respect and deference, and that tacit acknowledgment of his rights of manhood and government, which could not but be soothing and pleasant to one so afflicted. Or, perhaps—let us give the kindest interpretation possible to all things —the Earl's helplessness and loveableness touched a chord long silent, or never stirred before, in the heart of the man of the world. Possibly — who can say ? — he really began to like him.

At any rate, he seemed as if he did ; and Lord Cairnforth gave back to him in double measure all that he bestowed.

As a matter of course, all the Captain's pecuniary needs were at once supplied. His thread-bare clothes became mysteriously changed into a wardrobe supplied with every thing that a gentleman could desire, and a rather luxurious gentleman too ; which, owing to his Indian habits and his delicate health, the young Captain turned out to be. At first he resisted all this kindness; but all remonstrances being soon overcome, he took his luxuries quite naturally, and evidently enjoyed them — though scarcely so much as the Earl himself.

To that warm heart, which had never had half enough of ties whereon to expend itself and its wealth of generosity, it was perfectly delicious to see the sick soldier daily gaining health by riding the Cairnforth horses, shooting over the moors, or fishing in the lochs. Never had the Earl so keenly enjoyed his own wealth, and the blessings it enabled him to lavish abroad; never in his lifetime had he looked so thoroughly contented.

"Helen," he said one day when she had come up for an hour or two to the

Castle, and then, as usual, Captain Bruce had taken the opportunity of riding out: he owned he found Miss Cardross's company and conversation " slow " — " Helen, that young man looks stronger and better every day. What a bright-looking fellow he is! It does one good to see him."

And the Earl followed with his eyes the graceful steed, and equally graceful rider, caracoling in front of the Castle windows.

Helen said nothing.

" I think," he continued, " that the next best thing to being happy oneself is to be able to make other people so. Perhaps that may be the sort of happiness they have in the next world. I often speculate about it, and wonder what sort of creature I shall find myself there. — But," added he abruptly, " now to business. You will be my secretary instead of Bruce, this morning ? "

" Willingly." For though she too, like Malcolm, had been a little displaced by this charming cousin, there was not an atom of jealousy in her nature. Hers was that pure and unselfish affection which could bear to stand by and see those she loved made happy, even though it was by another than herself.

She fell to work in her old way, and the Earl employed as much as he required her ready handwriting, her clear head, and her full acquaintance with everybody and everything in the district. For Helen was a real minister's daughter — as popular and as necessary in the parish as the minister himself. And she was equally important at the Castle, where she was consulted, as this morning, on everything Lord Cairnforth was about to do, and on the wisest way of expending — he did not wish to save — the large yearly income which he now seemed really beginning to enjoy.

Helen, too, after a long morning's work, drew her breath with a sigh of pleasure.

"What a grand thing it is to be as rich as you are!"

"Why so?"

"One can do such a deal of good with plenty of money."

"Yes. Should you like to be very rich, Helen?"—watching her with an amused look.

Helen shook her head and laughed. "Oh, it's no use asking me the question, for I shall never have the chance of being rich."

"You cannot say; you might marry, for instance."

"That is not likely. Papa could never do without me; besides, as the folk say, I'm 'no bonnie, ye ken.' But," speaking more seriously, "indeed, I never think of marrying. If it is to be, it will be; if not, I am quite happy as I am. And for money, can I not always come to you whenever I want it? You supply me endlessly for my poor people. And as Captain Bruce was saying to papa the other night, you are a perfect mine of gold — and of generosity."

"Helen," Lord Cairnforth said, after he had sat thinking awhile, "I wanted to consult you about Captain Bruce. How do you like him? That is, do you still continue to like him, for I know you did at first?"

"And I do still. I feel so very sorry for him."

"Only, my dear," — Lord Cairnforth sometimes called her 'my dear,' and spoke to her with a tender, superior wisdom — "one's link to one's friends ought to be a little stronger than being sorry for them; one ought to respect them. One

must respect them before one can trust
them very much — with one's property for
instance."

"Do you mean," said straight forward
Helen, " that you have any thoughts of
making Captain Bruce your heir?"

"No, certainly not; but I have grave
doubts whether I ought not to remember
him in my will — only I wished to see
his health re-established first. Since, had
he continued as delicate as when he
came, he might not even have outlived
me."

"How calmly you talk of all this,"
said Helen, with a little shiver. She, full
of life and health, could hardly realise
the feeling of one who stood always
on the brink of another world, and

looking to that world only for real health — real life.

"I think of it calmly — and therefore speak calmly. But, dear Helen, I will not grieve you to-day. There is plenty of time; and all is safe whatever happens. I can trust my successor to do rightly. As for my cousin, I will try him a little longer, lest he prove

'A little more than kin, and less than kind.'"

"There seems no likelihood of that. He always speaks in the warmest manner of you whenever he comes to the Manse — that is what makes me like him, I fancy. And also, because I would always believe the best of people until I found out to the contrary. Life would not be worth having, if we were continually suspecting everybody; believing everybody bad till we had found them out to be good. If so, with many, I fear, we should never find the good out at all. That is — I can't put it cleverly, like you; but I know what I mean."

Lord Cairnforth smiled. "So do I, Helen, which is quite enough for us two. We will talk this over some other time; and meanwhile," — he looked at her earnestly and spoke with meaning — "if ever you have an opportunity of being kind to Captain Bruce, remember he is my next of kin, and I wish it."

"Certainly," answered Helen. "But I am never likely to have the chance of doing any kindness to such a very fine gentleman."

Lord Cairnforth smiled to himself once more, and let the conversation end; afterwards — long afterwards, he recalled it, and thought with a strange comfort that then at least there was nothing to conceal: nothing but sincerity in the sweet, honest face — not pretty, but so perfectly candid and true — with the sun shining on the lint-white hair, and the bright blue eyes meeting his, guileless as a child's. Ay, and however they were dimmed with care and washed with tears — oceans of bitterness — that innocent, child-like look never, even when she was an old woman, quite faded out of Helen's eyes.

"Ay," Lord Cairnforth said to himself, when she had gone away, and he was left alone in that helpless solitude which,

being the inevitable necessity, had grown
into the familiar habit of his life, " Ay,
it is all right. No harm could come —
there would be nothing neglected — even
were I to die to-morrow."

That " dying to - morrow " — which
might happen to any one of us — how
few really recognise it and prepare for it!
Not in the ordinary religious sense of
" preparation for death," — often a most
irreligious thing — a frantic attempt of
sinning and terror-stricken humanity to
strike a balance-sheet with heaven, just
leaving a sufficient portion on the credit
side ; — but preparation in the ordinary
worldly meaning — keeping one's affairs
straight and clear, that no one may be
perplexed therewith afterwards ; forgiving,

and asking forgiveness of offences ; removing evil done, and delaying not for a day any good that it is possible to do.

It was a strange thing ; but, as after his death it was discovered, the true secret of the wonderful calmness and sweetness which, year by year, deepened more and more in Lord Cairnforth's character, ripening it to a perfectness in which those who only saw the outside of his life could hardly believe—consisted in this ever-abiding thought — that he might die to-morrow. Existence was to him such a mere twilight, dim, imperfect, and sad, that he never rested in it, but lived every day, as it were, in the prospect of the eternal dawn.

Chapter the Ninth.

THIS summer, which, as it glided away, Lord Cairnforth often declared to be the happiest of his life, ended by bringing him the first heavy affliction — external affliction — which his life had ever known.

Suddenly, in the midst of the late-earned rest of a very toilsome career, died Mr. Menteith, the Earl's long-faithful friend, who had been almost as good to him as a father. He felt it sorely: the more so, because, though his own frail life seemed always under the imminent shadow of death,

death had never touched him before as regarded other people. He had lived, as we all unconsciously do, till the great enemy smites us, — feeling as if, whatever might be the case with himself, those whom he loved could never die. This grief was something quite new to him, and it struck him hard.

The tidings came on a gloomy day in late October: the season when Cairnforth is least beautiful, for the thick woods about it make the always damp atmosphere heavy with " the moist, rich smell of the rotting leaves," and the roads lying deep in mud, and the low shore hung with constant mists, give a general impression of dreariness. The far - away hills vanish entirely for days together, and the loch itself takes a leaden hue, as if it never could be blue again. You can hardly believe that the sun will ever again shine out upon it, the white waves rise, the mountains reappear, and the whole scene grow clear and lovely — as life does sometimes if we have only patience to endure· through the weary winter until spring.

But for the good man, John Menteith, his springs and winters were alike ended; he was gathered to his fathers, and his late ward mourned him bitterly.

Mr. Cardross and Helen, coming up to the Castle as soon as the news reached them, found Lord Cairnforth in a state of depression such as they had never before witnessed in him. One of the things which seemed to affect him most painfully, as small things sometimes do, in the midst of deepest grief, was that he could not attend Mr. Menteith's funeral.

"Every other man," said he, sadly, "every other man can follow his dear friends and kindred to the grave, can give them respect in death as he has given them love and help during life — I can do neither. I can help no one — be of use to no one. I am a mere cumberer of the ground. It would be better if I were away."

"Hush! do not dare to say that," answered Mr. Cardross. And he sent the rest away, even Helen, and sat down beside his old pupil, not merely as a friend, but as a minister — in the deepest meaning of the word, even as it was first used of

Him who "came not to be ministered unto, but to minister."

Helen's father was not a demonstrative man under ordinary circumstances; he was too much absorbed in his books, and in a sort of languid indifference to worldly matters which had hung over him, more or less, ever since his wife's death. But when occasion arose he could rise equal to it. And he was one of those comforters who knew the way through the valley of affliction by the marks which their own feet have trod.

He and the Earl spent a whole hour alone together. Afterwards, when sorrow, compared with which the present grief was calm and sacred, fell upon them both, they remembered this day, and were not afraid to open their wounded hearts to one another.

At last, Mr. Cardross came out of the library, and told Helen that Lord Cairnforth wanted to speak to her.

" He wishes to have your opinion, as well as my own, about a journey he is projecting to Edinburgh, and some business matters which he desires to arrange there. I think he would have liked to see Captain Bruce, too. Where is he ? "

The Captain had found this atmosphere of sorrow a little too overpowering, and had disappeared for a long ride. So Miss Cardross had been sitting alone all the time.

" Your father has been persuading me,

Helen," said the Earl, when she came in, "that I am not quite so useless in the world as I imagined. He says, he has reason to believe, from things Mr. Menteith let fall, that my dear old friend's widow is not very well provided for, and she and her children will have a hard battle even now. Mr. Cardross thinks I can help her very materially. In one way especially. You know I have made my will?"

"Yes," replied unconscious Helen, "you told me so."

"Mr. Menteith drew it up the last time he was here. How little we thought it would be really the last time! Ah, Helen, if we could only look forward!"

"It is best not," said Helen, earnestly.

"Well, my will is made. And though

in it I left nothing to Mr. Menteith himself, seeing that such a return of his kindness would be very unwelcome, I insisted on doing what was equivalent: bequeathing a thousand pounds to each of his children. Was I right in that? You do not object?"

"Most assuredly not," answered Helen, though a little surprised at the question. Still, she was so long accustomed to be consulted by the Earl, and to give her opinion frankly and freely on all points, that the surprise was only momentary.

"And, by the way, I mean to leave the same sum — one thousand pounds — to my cousin, Captain Bruce. Remember that, Helen: remember it particularly, will you? in case anything should happen before I have time to add this to my will. But, to the Mentciths. Your father thinks, and I agree with him, that the money I design for them will be far better spent now, or some portion of it, in helping these fatherless children on in the world, than in keeping them waiting for my death, which may not happen for years. What do you think?"

Helen agreed heartily. It would cause a certain diminution of yearly income, but then the Earl had far more than enough for his own wants, and if not spent thus, the sum would certainly have been expended by him in some other form of benevolence. She said as much.

" Possibly it might. What else should I do with it ? " was Lord Cairnforth's answer. " But, in order to get at the

 A Noble Life.

money, and alter my will, so that in no case should this sum be paid twice over, to the injury of my heir — I must take care of my heir," and he slightly smiled, "I ought to go at once to Edinburgh. Shall I?"

Helen hesitated. The Earl's last journey had been so unpropitious — he had taken so long a time to recover from it — that she had earnestly hoped he would never attempt another. She expressed this, as delicately as she could.

" No — I never would have attempted it for myself. Change is only pain and weariness to me. I have no wish to leave dear, familiar Cairnforth, till I leave it for—the place where my good old friend is now. And sometimes, Helen, I fancy the hills of Paradise will not be very unlike the hills about our loch. You would think of me far away, when you were looking at them sometimes?"

Helen fixed her tender eyes upon him — "It is quite as likely that you may have to think of me thus, for I may go first; I am the elder of us two. But all that is in God's hands alone. About Edinburgh now. When do you start?"

"At once, I think: though with my slow travelling I should not be in time for the funeral; and even if I were, I could not attend it without giving much trouble to other people. But — as your father has shown me — the funeral does not signify. The great matter is to be of use to Mrs. Menteith and the children in the way I explained. Have I your consent, my dear?"

For answer, Helen pointed to a few lines in a Bible which lay open on the library table: no doubt her father had been reading out of it — for it was open at that portion which seems to have plumbed the depth of all human anguish — the Book of Job. She repeated the verses —

" ' When the ear heard me, then it blessed me: and when the eye saw me, it gave witness to me:

" ' Because I delivered the poor that cried, and the fatherless, and him that had none to help him:

" ' The blessing of him that was ready to perish came upon me, and I caused the widow's heart to sing for joy.'

" That is what will be said of you,

one day, Lord Cairnforth. Is not this something worth living for?"

"Ay, it is!" replied the Earl, deeply moved — and Helen was scarcely less so.

They discussed no more the journey to Edinburgh; but Lord Cairnforth, in his decided way, gave orders immediately to prepare for it — taking with him, as usual, Malcolm and Mrs. Campbell. By the time Captain Bruce returned from his ride, the guest was startled by the news that his host meant to quit Cairnforth at daylight the next morning; which appeared to disconcert the Captain exceedingly.

"I would volunteer to accompany you, cousin," said, he, after expressing his extreme surprise and regret, "but the winds of Edinburgh are ruin to my weak

lungs, which the air here suits so well.
So I must prepare to quit pleasant Cairnforth, where I have received so much
kindness, and which I have grown to
regard almost like home — the nearest
approach to home that in my sad, wandering life I ever knew."

There was an unmistakeable regret in the
young man's tone, which, in spite of his own
trouble, went to the Earl's good heart.

"Why should you leave at all?" said
he. "Why not remain here and await
my return, which cannot be long delayed?
— two months at most — even counting
my slow travelling. I will give you
something to do meanwhile: — I will make
you viceroy of Cairnforth during my absence
— that is, under Miss Cardross, who alone

knows all the parish affairs — and mine. Will you accept the office?"

"Under Miss Cardross?" Captain Bruce laughed — but did not seem quite to relish it. However, he expressed much gratitude at having been thought worthy of the Earl's confidence.

"Don't be humble, my good cousin and friend. If I did not trust you, and like you, I should never think of asking you to stay. Mr. Cardross — Helen — what do you say to my plan?"

Both gave a cordial assent: as was indeed certain. Nothing ill was known of Captain Bruce, and nothing noticed in him unlikeable, or unworthy of liking. And even as to his family, who wrote to him constantly, and whose letters he

often showed, there had appeared sufficient evidence in their favour to counter-
balance much of the suspicions against
them: so that the Earl was glad he
had leaned to the charitable side in
making his cousin welcome to Cairnforth.
Glad, too, that he could atone by warm
confidence and extra kindness for what
now seemed too long a neglect of those
who were really his nearest kith and
kin.

Mr. Cardross, also: any prejudices he
had from his knowledge of the late Earl's
troubles with the Bruces were long ago
dispersed. And Helen was too innocent
herself ever to have had a prejudice at
all. She said, when appealed to, pointedly,
by the Earl, as he now often appealed to

her in many things, — that she thought the scheme both pleasant and advisable.

"And now, papa," added she, for her watchful eye detected Lord Cairnforth's pale face and wearied air, "let us say good-night — and good-bye."

Long after, they remembered, all of them, what an exceedingly quiet and ordinary good-bye it was — none having the slightest feeling that it was more than a temporary parting. The whole thing had been so sudden, that the day's events appeared quite shadowy—and as if everybody would wake up to-morrow morning to find them nothing but a dream.

Besides, there was a little hurrying and confusion consequent on the Earl's insisting on sending the Cardrosses home, for the dull, calm day had changed into the wildest of nights — one of those sudden equinoctial storms that in an hour or two alter the whole aspect of things in this region.

"You must take the carriage, Helen — you and your father; it is the last thing I can do for you — and I would do everything in the world for you if I could; but I shall, one day. Good-bye. Take care of yourself, my dear."

These were the Earl's farewell words to her. She was so accustomed to his goodness and kindness that she never thought much about them; till long afterwards, when kindness was gone, and goodness seemed the merest delusion and dream.

When his friends had departed, Lord Cairnforth sat silent and melancholy. His cousin good-naturedly tried to rouse him into the usual contest at chess with which they had begun to while away the long winter evenings, and which just suited Lord Cairnforth's acute, accurate, and introspective brain, accustomed to plan and to order — so that he delighted in the game, and was soon as good a player as his teacher. But now his mind was disturbed and restless — he sat by the fireside, listening to the fierce wind that went howling round and round the Castle, as the wind can howl along the sometimes placid shores of Loch Beg.

"I hope they have reached the Manse in safety. Let me know, Malcolm, when the carriage returns. I will go to bed then. I wish they would have remained

here; but the minister never will stay —
he dislikes sleeping a single night from
under his own roof. Is he not a good
man, cousin — one of a thousand?"

"I have not the slightest doubt of it."

"And his daughter — have you in any
way modified your opinion of her, which
at first was not very favourable?"

"Not as to her beauty, certainly," was
the careless reply. "She's 'no bonnie,'
as you say in these parts — terribly
Scotch; but she is very good. Only
don't you think good people are just a
little wearisome sometimes?"

The Earl smiled. He was accustomed
to, and often rather amused by, his
cousin's honest worldlinesses and outspoken
scepticisms — that candid confession of bad-

ness which always inclines a kindly heart to believe the very best of the penitent.

"Nevertheless, though Miss Cardross may be 'no bonnie,' and too good to please your taste, I hope you will go often to the Manse in my absence, and write me word how they are. Otherwise I shall hear little — the minister's letters are too voluminous to be frequent—and Miss Cardross is not given to much correspondence."

Captain Bruce promised, and again the two young men sat silent, listening to the eerie howling of the wind. It inclined both of them to graver talk than was their habit when together.

"I wonder," said the Earl, "whether this blast, according to popular superstition, is come to carry many souls away with it 'on the wings of the wind!' Where will they fly to the instant they leave the body? How free and happy they must feel!"

"What an odd fancy! and not a particularly pleasant one," replied the Captain with a shiver.

"Not unpleasant, to my mind. I like to think of these things. If I were out of the body, I should, if I could, fly back to Cairnforth."

"Pray don't imagine such dreadful things. May you live a hundred years!"

"Not quite, I hope. A hundred years —of *my* life! No. The most loving friend I have would not wish it for me." Then, suddenly, as with an impulse created by the sad events of the day—the stormy night—

and the disturbed state of his own mental condition, inclining him to any sort of companionship, " Cousin, I am going to trust you — specially; in a matter of business which I wish named to the Cardrosses. I should have done so before they left to-night. May I confide to you the message?"

"Willingly. What is it about?" and the Captain's keen, black eyes assumed an expression which, if the Earl had noticed, he might have repented of his trust. But no, he never would have noticed it. His upright, honest nature — though capable of great reserve — was utterly incapable of false pretences, deceit, or self-interested diplomacy. And what was impossible in himself he never suspected in other people. He thought his cousin shallow sometimes, but good-natured; a little worldly perhaps, but always well-meaning. That Captain Bruce could have come to Cairnforth for any purpose but mere curiosity, and remained there for any motive except idleness and the pursuit of health, did not occur to Lord Cairnforth.

"It is on the subject that you so much dislike my talking about — my own death; a probability which I have to consider; as being rather nearer to me than it is to most people. Should I die, will you remember that my will lies at the office of Menteith and Ross, Edinburgh?"

"So you have made your will?" said the Captain, rather eagerly; then added, "What a courageous man you are! I never durst make mine. But then, to be sure, I have nothing to leave — except my sword, which I hereby make over to you, well-beloved cousin."

"Thank you, though I should have very little use for it. And that reminds me to explain something. The day I made my will was, by an odd chance, the day you arrived here. Had I known you then, I should have named you in it, leaving you—I may as well tell you the sum—a' thousand pounds, in token of cousinly regard."

"You are exceedingly kind, but I am no fortune-hunter."

"I know that. Still, the legacy may not be useless. I shall make it legally secure as soon as I get to Edinburgh. In any case you are quite safe, for I have mentioned you to my heir."

"Your heir! whom do you mean?" interrupted Captain Bruce, thrown off his guard by excessive surprise.

The Earl said, with a little dignity of manner, "It is scarcely needful to answer your question. The title, you are aware, will be extinct; I meant the successor to my landed property."

"Do I know the gentleman?"

"I named no gentleman."

"Not surely a lady? Not—" a light suddenly breaking in upon him, so startling that it overthrew all his self-control, and even his good breeding. "It cannot possibly be Miss Helen Cardross?"

"Captain Bruce," said the Earl, the angry colour flashing all over his pale face, "I was simply communicating a message to you — there was no need for any further questioning."

"I beg your pardon, Lord Cairnforth," returned the other, perceiving how great a mistake he had made. "I have no right whatever to question or even to speculate concerning your heir, who is doubtless the fittest person you could have selected."

"Most certainly," replied the Earl, in a manner which put a final stop to the conversation.

It was not resumed on any other topics; and shortly afterwards, Malcolm having come in with the announcement that the carriage had returned from the Manse (at which Captain Bruce's sharp eyes were bent scrutinisingly on the Earl's face, but learnt nothing thence), the cousins separated.

The Captain had faithfully promised to be up at dawn to see the travellers off, but an apology came from him to the effect that the morning air was too damp for his lungs, and that he had spent a sleepless night owing to his cough.

"An' nae wonder," remarked Malcolm cynically, as he delivered the message. "For I heard him a' through the wee hours, walkin' and walkin' up and doun, for a' the warld like a wolf in a cage. And eh, but he's dour the day!"

"A sickly man finds it difficult not to be dour at times," said the Earl of Cairnforth.

END OF THE FIRST VOLUME.